Once Upon a Street

Norfolk Stories for Children

To Abbi

Isabelle King

Wow!

Best wishes x

ONCE UPON A STREET

NORFOLK STORIES FOR CHILDREN

ISABELLE KING

ILLUSTRATED BY JOHN MCKEEVER

First published 2019

The History Press
The Mill, Brimscombe Port
Stroud, Gloucestershire, GL5 2QG
www.thehistorypress.co.uk

British Library Cataloguing in Publication Data.
A catalogue record for this book is available from the British Library.

ISBN 978 0 7509 8989 3

Typesetting and origination by The History Press
Printed in Great Britain

CONTENTS

Isabelle King
(Wolf Marloh Photography)

INTRODUCTION
AND THANK YOUS

Every street has a story. To discover that story, all you have to do is step back in time; just imagine, you pop to the shop or the park and on your way along the high street, everything changes. The shops and supermarkets vanish and in their place are market stalls and street vendors. There are no cars or buses; all around you people walk or ride horses, and you are swept up in the lively hustle and bustle of this busy day. As for that roundabout, it disappears and in its place stands an enormous stone arch decorated with Tudor roses. Through the arch, riding a horse, comes a queen wearing a magnificent dress with swirly gold patterns. You have travelled back to the time of Elizabethan history where a great royal procession happened on this street, the very same street where you go shopping! The street where you go for walks by the river was once a medieval port where you can see the boats whipping over the waves and smell the sea salt on the air, bitter as the stormy wind. The street you walk along to get to the theatre was once filled with the dainty footsteps of the elegant Georgian gentry, off to one of their dazzling parties: see that Georgian lady with her fancy dress and enormous wig, swirling up and up like a big whirl of ice cream. In Norfolk, the streets are rich with such stories; delve into the region's history and you will be sure to discover something wondrous – a magical marketplace, a factory for fairground animals, a spectacular circus or a marvellous home for a mighty dragon.

Streets, much like stories, bring people together. Look at a map and the ways the streets connect communities; well, stories do that too. Much like a storyline, the roads of a street may weave and wind in different directions but they still connect people with each other. Now, there's lots to learn when you step back in time – so many things are different – the places, the buildings, the people, their way of life … yikes, that's rather a lot of information to take on board! If only there were some special place where historical information was collected together in a fun and interesting way. Ah yes, enter museums, heritage centres and libraries! Norfolk Heritage Centre, for example, was my main source of information for this book. Norfolk Heritage Centre is on the second floor of Norfolk and Norwich Millennium Library, and it houses many fascinating archives of books, maps and items relating to Norfolk history. It was very exciting to discover how much of that history is linked with the arts and popular entertainment, and so this book has a theatrical theme.

As people are at the heart of these stories, love and friendship take centre stage.

This is the third book I've written inspired by Norfolk history and it's been the most incredible adventure. *The Norfolk Story Book* is inspired by objects at Norfolk Collections Centre, a museum on site at Gressenhall Farm and Workhouse – the book saw me researching mammoths, mustard, snapdragons, toffee and Christmas crackers!

Once Upon A Time in Norfolk is inspired by museums throughout Norfolk Museums Service, which saw me researching the Norman knights of Norwich Castle, the enchanting weavers of Strangers' Hall, the adventurous Iceni of Roman Britain and many more. What really draws me to the history is the thought not just of the place but also of the people who lived there, not just the object but the person who used it. Sometimes, not much is known about the people. That's where writers come in and we make up stories about what might have happened. With that in mind, it's important to note that some things in this book are based on historical truth and some things are made up.

There are three parts to making this historical story. Part one, I decide what I'm going to write about. This involves looking through the archives at Norfolk Heritage Centre and choosing items, for example circus posters from the Victorian era, a map of Norwich from Elizabethan times and an article from a newspaper of the Georgian era. Part two, I root the story in history by doing research. Research is fantastically interesting and mainly involves asking questions to the helpful staff at Norfolk Heritage Centre and sticking my nose in history books for days on end. Part three, I make up the story! This involves imagining the characters and situations to make the story magical and exciting. It's rather like putting the final layer on a cake – this is the fun, playful layer with all the fancy icing and sprinkles. Speaking of cakes, I particularly enjoyed researching the delicious treats of the Georgian era, plenty of cakes were sampled for serious research purposes. As the Georgians loved their fashion, I thought it would be a good idea to include fabulous footnotes with fabulous shoes. The fabulous footnotes accompany each story to highlight the historical places and objects that inspired me to write. And of course, it doesn't have to end there for you; if you enjoy learning about local history and love to get creative, why not make up your own story about a street?

I believe we are all storytellers and there are many ways that you might like to tell *your* story: writing, drawing pictures, playing music, performing, acting, singing, dancing, designing costumes, the list could go on and on; different types of art and creativity are different types of storytelling. That's why reading is so brilliant because it opens up whole worlds of imagination and, in turn, helps us to get ideas for all the fantastic things we are going to do in the future.

I would like to give special thanks to the wonderful staff at Norfolk Heritage Centre, and in particular a huge thank you to Chris Tracy and Rachel Ridealgh for being so kind, helpful and full of knowledge.

Many thanks to the amazing staff at Norfolk Museums Service for all your support. Abundant thanks to Dr John Davies for your support and infinite knowledge.

I would also like to thank the lovely staff at Norfolk and Norwich Millennium Library where I had the pleasure of being Writer in Residence for the duration of their British Library exhibition, 'Quentin Blake: The Roald Dahl Centenary Portraits'. Thank you to The British Library for your support and kindness. Thank you to The Prince's Trust for being amazing and believing in me. It's been an honour to be a Young Ambassador for The Prince's Trust.

Thank you to my wonderful publisher The History Press, it's a real pleasure to write these books. Take a bow, illustrator John McKeever, I couldn't be more delighted with seeing the characters come to life with such vibrant illustrations – you big legend.

Thank you lovely family, love you Mum and Dad. We've had some lovely days out seeing some of the sites in this book!

Finally, reader, I would like to thank you for reading this book. I hope you enjoy reading it – I wrote it for you! Now, the characters are waiting in the wings to perform for you. It's time to raise the curtain. The stage is set: let's get lost in some Norfolk magic.

1

TA-DA! THE DAZZLING DANCER OF THEATRE ROYAL

Excited audience, take to your seats
Tonight you are in for wonderful treats
Everyone claps as the curtain rises,
A spectacular show of wondrous surprises.
It's him! Here he is with a rat-a-tat-ta-da!
The dazzling dancer of Theatre Royal – horah!
You'll be happy you ventured to Theatre Street
to see this performer so quick on his feet
Soft as spun sugar, light as whipped cream
each twizzle, each twirl to behold is a dream
An elegant, exquisite, excellent prancer
Norwich's very own mysterious masked dancer

Yes, he is disguised in theatrical mask
But who is he really? The audience ask
Who indeed? Let's find out
because that's what this story is all about
How a boy from nowhere became a star of the stage
Discover his journey with each turn of the page
The start of the tale is the end of this rhyme
And so it begins with once upon a time …

Once upon a time there lived a boy called Fred. Just Fred, nothing else. Just Fred nothing else lived in a time called the Georgian era when King George sat on the throne. There were four King Georges and Fred lived in the time of George III. Step back into this time and you would be sure to notice how fancy it was. The Georgians wore very fine and beautiful clothes, dresses of splendid silk and luxurious lace. Their heads were decorated with great big wigs which swirled up and up like enormous whirls of cream and as for their feet, *fabulous shoes*!

The Georgians loved a good party and really knew how to put on a feast with delicious teas, fruits, pastries, custards and cakes. These were not the sort of cakes you would just guzzle and chomp down in one go; oh no, these cakes were works of art to be admired, with neat layers of soft sponge and delicate drizzles of sugars and cherries, often called *dainties* and *fancies* – to be scoffed in a dainty, fancy way, if you please. Magnificent balls were all the fashion, a chance to dress up, eat, drink and dance to the pleasant sounds of harmonious harps, tooting flutes, flitting lutes and pretty pianos. Fine music, big wigs, marzipan and jelly galore, you could have all this and more, right outside your door, provided, that is, on one vital score, the good luck of which you had been born extremely ... rich!

Being rich meant you were a member of the gentlefolk, or 'gentry', in the finest clothes you ever saw. And guess what? Fred was not. Rags and tatters, that's what Fred wore. Now there are three things you need to know about Fred. The first, as we have discovered, is that

he didn't have much to call his own. Fred
lived on the streets of Norwich with no home,
no family and no one but himself to rely on.
He had a handful of pennies to his name; one
of the pennies had holes in it and might have
been an old button for all Fred knew.

The second thing you need to know is that
while Fred didn't have a person to rely on he
did have a pet, a tiny puppy called Pebbles.
Pebbles was a mischievous little scrap of a
scamp with a keen nose, alert eyes and a teeny,
twitching tail. Fred had named him Pebbles
because the way he constantly skipped up and
down, ever so lightly, reminded him of pebbles
as they skimmed across the water. Fred had
found Pebbles on an evening swagger down
by the River Wensum. Some old wooden
boxes were piled up against a wall and one of
them was rattling about. No sooner had Fred
opened the box than out rolled a stray puppy,
straight into his arms as though it had always
belonged there. Considerate and sensitive of
nature, Fred decided to take care of this tiny
scruff of fluff. Besides, that pup had the sort

of look that said if he didn't cause trouble he would tumble into it one way or another and so, thought Fred, someone's got to keep an eye on the little rascal.

The third thing you need to know about Fred is that he was a fantastic dancer. Delicate as sunlight filters through the trees, nimble as a robin goes bobbin' on the breeze, Fred could dance you into a daydream. You see, Fred desperately needed a way to earn money and since he had rather a natural flair for being quick on his feet, he had decided he would do this by dancing. The idea was to impress passers-by with his dancing skills and hopefully they would throw a few coins his way. Now, to get people's attention, he couldn't just be good, he had to be *amazing*. And so Fred practised and practised and practised to the point that it would indeed, appear to a passer-by that the boy was so talented it couldn't be natural and must be magic. Fred, however, would soon correct them. 'Everyone has a gift, something special and unique about them, but a gift doesn't just become the best it could be without any work. The secret to my skills isn't magic. It's practice!' Fred would happily tell this to anyone who cared to watch.

The problem was that no one did care to watch. 'Get out of the way, street boy!' people yelled at him. 'Move over, street boy, out of my way!'

'No time for you, street boy, stop prancing about!'

It seemed to Fred that no matter how delightful his dancing, he could never get the audience he deserved. Until one morning, warm and sunny, Fred woke up with a funny feeling in his tummy: it felt like butterflies fluttering about as though something different that day would surely come about.

Pebbles bounded up to Fred with something in his mouth, which he presented at his feet with pride as though it were a trophy. It was a crumpled copy of *The Norfolk Chronicle*. Fred had been taught slowly how to read by a kind schoolmistress who helped street children. They had read little bits of *The Norfolk Chronicle* together every day and, much like his dancing, Fred found that the more he practised, the better he got. Not only that but he had got to know *The Norfolk Chronicle* very well, a useful paper which let you know about important things happening in the area. Pebbles always went to see if there was a spare copy he could pick up in the morning. The little pup placed his paw on an article and barked and wagged his tail until Fred looked at it. As Pebbles lifted his paw, Fred read words that sent tingles of excitement down his spine:

AT THE THEATRE-ROYAL

By His MAJESTY'S Servants

THIS prefent Evening, July 22, will
be presented a comedy, call'd
The BEGGAR'S OPERA
To which will be added,
WIT'S LAST STAKE

To begin at Half an Hour
after Six o'Clock.

Tickets to be had of Mr. Griffith,
at his Houfe opposite
St Stephen's Church; of Mr Croufe,
and at Mr Sutton's
Peruke-maker, in the Market-place;
and of Mr Smith
at his office at the Theatre.

'A show at the theatre,' marvelled Fred. 'What a wonderful idea! I could go and see what the performers are like. Then perhaps one day I could audition to be on stage. If I was up there on the big stage people would definitely pay to see me dance. Oh, well done for bringing me this, Pebbles, you clever thing!' Fred rubbed Pebbles' tummy and the little pup rolled over yapping as if to say, 'Yes, I am clever, Fred, thank you!'

Fred had never set foot in the Theatre Royal before, though he loved to see the building. He knew it was built by a man called Thomas Ivory and he much admired this master builder as a person who had used his talents to make his way in the world. A few years earlier, on the very same street, Thomas Ivory had also built a lovely, grand building called the Assembly Rooms. Fred wasn't allowed to go inside the Assembly Rooms because he wasn't a member of the gentry. The Assembly Rooms were a perfect place for the gentry to get together and have parties, balls, play cards, enjoy fun, frolics and fine food. There was even a lawn outside for playing bowls. Fred would often watch the gentry with fascination as they entered the Assembly Rooms, all dressed up in their glittering finest. The fact he wasn't allowed inside the building meant that he was all the more intrigued by it. As for the theatre … well, Fred had seen people in rags and tatters go to the theatre and that meant he could go in too. Fred went to Mr Smith at his office and spent every penny he had (including the button) on a ticket. That night, at half an hour past six o'clock, darkness drew in like a velvet curtain, a pale moon glowed brightly and stars twinkled cheekily as though they were telling each other secrets. Fred and Pebbles joined the crowd of people entering Norwich Theatre Royal. The first thing that struck Fred was how unusual it was to see the gentry and people just like him all inside the same building. The theatre must be a very powerful place, he thought, to bring people together like this.

The shows were very vibrant and funny. *The Begger's Opera* had lots of singing in it and the actors had wonderful voices. *Wit's Last Stake* was a farce, a very fast comedy. Some bits in both shows were a bit grown-up and Fred couldn't always understand what was happening, but he enjoyed the performances.

'You know what this show needs, Pebbles,' he said, 'more dancing! That could be me up there on stage. I just need to find a way to get on stage. Oh, there must be a way …'

After the show, Fred twirled outside of the theatre, Pebbles hopping after him.

'I'm the Dazzling Dancer of Theatre Royal' Fred sang to himself. 'Tonight, ladies and gentleman, you are about to watch … now don't lose your wits and hold on to your wigs, you are about to watch … the Dazzling Dancer of Theatre Royal!'

He was so much in a beautiful daydream that he didn't notice he was waltzing straight into a bustling crowd of people gathered outside the Assembly Rooms on the same street. It was the gentry, all dressed up in fancy dress, some as pirates, some as princesses, some as rogues and vagabonds. Everyone wore a theatrical mask. They were going to have a masked ball, or 'masquerade', inside the Assembly Rooms. Fred accidentally bumped into a gentleman who was wearing rather a dark mask with the mouth turned downwards, an unhappy face. As he bumped into him Fred knocked something out of the gentleman's hands, though he didn't see what it was.

'Oh sorry, Sir,' gasped Fred. The gentleman said nothing but turned his back to Fred and walked away. On the back of his head was another mask with the mouth turned upwards, a happy face. Fred couldn't help but laugh.

'Looks like all these people are off to have a fun time. Now you stay close to me, Pebbles,' he instructed his puppy, 'I know what you're like, anything exciting and shiny and you just wander off. You stay right by my side and don't even think about … don't … Pebbles, Pebbles, where are you?'

Fred looked anxiously up and down until at last he clapped eyes on that tiny wagging tail. To his horror Fred saw that the mischievous little scruff of fluff was gallivanting merrily about among the gentry as though he'd been invited. Being so small, it seemed that no one had noticed him yet. Pebbles had that determined look on his little face, his keen eyes fixed on the Assembly Rooms. 'No, Pebbles!' Fred yelled. 'You mustn't go inside, we're not allowed in there, you'll get into all sorts of trouble if they see you. Come back, Pebbles, come back!'

But Pebbles did not come back. On he scampered, slipping nimbly through the pitter-patter of hundreds of pretty shoes until he had disappeared into the building. Fred gulped and his heart pounded in his chest. He couldn't go inside. But he couldn't leave Pebbles to get into trouble! Whatever was he to do? As if in answer to his question, his feet kicked something on the ground.

Fred looked down and saw what he had accidentally knocked out of the gentleman's hands. It was a mask. The mask glittered bright gold; it was very beautiful. In his panic, Fred didn't stop to think. He picked up the mask and put it on his face. And, just like that, Fred fitted in.

After all, if people were dressed as rogues and vagabonds, Fred's rags and tatters could have just been a fancy-dress costume. And so Fred entered the Assembly Rooms. It was like stepping inside a slice of cake. Soft colours of creamy peach, buttery gold and velvety red swathed the walls around him. The room was flooded with people, chatting, laughing and having a jolly good time. Fred had to make an effort to stop his jaw from dropping when he saw all that food. Plates piled high with such delicious delights as he had never seen, and the drinks flowed and sparkled. Fred's mouth watered and his stomach rumbled ... perhaps he could have just ... one ... cake ... but no! He couldn't get distracted. 'Just find Pebbles and get out of here,' Fred urged himself. 'You can't risk being discovered.'

Fred darted his eyes frantically around the room for Pebbles and caught sight of something very curious. A floating pine apple? (Back then it was spelled as two words: pine apple.) Fred had never seen a real pine apple before, though he knew what it was because he had seen large stone statues outside grand buildings. Pine apples were expensive and exotic fruit, only very well-to-do people could have them and they used them as a symbol of how important they were: an exquisite prickly pine apple to show off your exquisite prickly importance. Fred was sure, however, that no matter how high and mighty the pine apple, that didn't mean it could float! He lowered his eyes and saw that the pine apple sat on top of a very tall stack of food with all sorts of dainty treats layered on top of each other: fancy cakes, fruits, custards and jellies, even the jellies seemed to wobble with a certain elegance.

Holding up the pile of food was a plate and holding up the plate was … Pebbles! Yes, Pebbles had disguised himself by carrying an enormous plate of food on his back, and as the plate passed through the crowds, people were so content with helping themselves to snacks that they didn't notice the puppy underneath. Fred rolled his eyes and was about to creep towards Pebbles and get that puppy out of the building when all of a sudden, he heard … *the music.* It was like the sound of spring when all the flowers burst into life. Up and down, up and down went the sound of violin strings, so lively yet gentle it reminded Fred of gushing water and sweeping fields with leaping lambs.

Fred had spent many years dancing on the streets without music, and he had never heard a sound like this before. Every part of him tingled, entranced. All of a sudden, Pebbles and the need to leave were forgotten. Fred felt *the music*. Fred felt *the moves*. They flowed though him like *magic*. Fred began to dance. His feet tapped against the floor, rat-a-tat-tat-tat-tat! His arms swept gracefully above his head. In time to those springing strings he skipped quickly up and down, weaving his way though people, light as though he were floating on air. Fred glided into a space on the ballroom floor and began to twirl round and round and round and round and round and … all of a sudden the music stopped.

Fred stopped. With his arms above his head, one leg poised on tiptoes, one hovering in mid air, Fred suddenly saw that he was surrounded by masked people. They had formed a circle around him and stood staring through their masks with astonishment. The room was silent. And then came a noise, a noise that he had never heard before, it started slowly then gradually grew louder and louder until the whole room was buzzing with this noise. It was a round of applause.

'Splendid!' people cried as they clapped their hands. 'Magnificent, wonderful, did you ever see such dancing?'

Fred had never had an audience before. It felt incredible. He gave a low bow, twirling his arms with a flourish. 'More, more,' the spellbound audience chanted. 'More, more!' The music struck up into a jolly jig. Invigorated by the enthusiasm all around him, Fred began to dance once more, even faster this time. How did he do it? No one knew but the boy had a gift, by golly that was true. Pebbles, eager to join in and still carrying the enormous plate of food on his back, bobbed his way through the crowds and joyfully tried to interweave between Fred's feet. Fred, alarmed that he would trip over the silly pup, bent down and gently picked up the plate, an action which he was surprised to find received another round of applause.

'Oh, marvellous,' his adoring fans cried. 'He's going to do a balancing act as part of his dance.'

'Crumbs!' thought Fred, 'I guess that means I'll have to do a balancing act as part of my dance.'

He span round and round, balancing the plate on one hand, the pine apple on top bouncing lightly up and down as he turned. This received another hearty round of applause. Pebbles watched happily, swaying his tiny tail from side to side, caught up in the rhythm. When the music stopped Fred finished his dance with an elaborate bow and placed the plate on the floor. His audience were ecstatic. 'Fantastic! Bravo!'

A very elegant lady stepped forward. She had a sparkling crystal mask and a wig as big as the pine apple. She curtseyed to Fred, lowered her mask and batted a dainty fan in front of her face. 'That was simply enchanting' she said. 'The way you moved, it was magic!'

'Thank you,' smiled Fred. He wasn't used to speaking to the gentry and felt rather nervous so the words came out only as a whisper.

'My name is Lady Pomplepuff,' the lady said, 'and I would love for you to dance at my parties in future. Now please, you must tell us who you are.'

'Who am I?' Fred repeated in shock. But of course! No one knew who he was. Dancing had felt like a happy daydream but in that moment, Fred came crashing back down to earth. The only reason he had an audience was because he was wearing a mask. No one ever wanted to watch him when he was on the streets. He wasn't even supposed to be in the Assembly Rooms at all. No matter what, he mustn't take off his mask, he mustn't let them find out that he was Fred, just Fred, nothing else. Time to make up a theatrical name!

'I'm, erm … I'm, um …' Fred stumbled at the sight of his audience politely waiting for an answer to a simple question. 'I'm, ummmmm …' suddenly Fred remembered the name he had given himself outside the Theatre Royal. 'I'm the Dazzling Dancer of Theatre Royal,' he cried and tapped his feet against the floor 'Rat-a-tat-tat-ta-da!'

'Bravo!' the audience clapped.

'What superb showmanship!' said Lady Pomplepuff. 'But, my good fellow, I simply must know who you really are! Why don't you take off your mask and show us? Go on, please, show us who you are.'

'Take off your mask,' the audience chanted. 'Take off your mask, take off your mask!'

Fred's heart pounded with panic. How was he going to get out of this?

'Take off your mask. Take off your mask.'

Fred looked desperately down at Pebbles, hoping the little puppy could help him somehow. Pebbles's tiny eyes narrowed determinedly as if to say he was on the case, and he scurried off. Then, all of a sudden, at the other end of the room, Fred saw another enormous plate of food topped with a pine apple rise into the air.

'Look! Over there! A floating pine apple!'

Everyone looked to where Fred had suddenly pointed, giving him time to dash away from the scene, yet another extraordinary use of his speed and lightness of touch. Befuddled as to what they were supposed to be looking at and why, the audience turned back only to find that …

'He's gone! Vanished! He really must be magic!' This was an exciting end to a highly entertaining evening. The room was alive with chatter. 'Wasn't he sensational? The way he danced! How did he do it?' No one knew, but the boy had a gift, by golly that was true. As for the floating pine apple, it snuck its way quietly out of the building. But no one noticed. They were all too busy talking about the Dazzling Dancer of Theatre Royal. The magic, the myth, the mystery behind the mask!

After that it was all 'It's him! There he is! Horah!' The Dazzling Dancer of Theatre Royal would pop up on street corners and perform for crowds which quickly gathered, gentry and streetfolk alike. Pebbles would walk through the crowds with a cap in his mouth to collect coins. Lady Pomplepuff was a huge fan and would often get lots of her very fashionable friends together to watch him perform on the streets. 'Oh, isn't he just charming?' Pebbles loved Lady Pomplepuff because she was kind and friendly; he jumped into her arms whenever he saw her. She adored him in turn and always brought some tasty scraps for him to eat.

And no matter what, Fred never took off his mask. He only removed it when he was alone in a quiet spot. And just like that, he went back to being Fred, just Fred, nothing else. Now, one day someone placed something in Pebbles's cap that wasn't a coin. It was something even better: a letter. Fred and Pebbles read it together when they were alone that evening. The letter was from His Majesty's Servants, an invitation for the Dazzling Dancer of Theatre Royal to perform at the building that inspired his name: the Theatre Royal. A special seat would be reserved for the performer's small fluffy companion. Fred was beside himself with excitement. 'Oh, Pebbles, this is it! I've found a way! A way to get up there on stage. If this goes well I might be allowed to always perform at The Theatre Royal.'

When the big day finally arrived, however, Fred's excitement had turned to utter nerves.

'Oh Pebbles, I'm terrified, I feel like my legs have turned to jelly. I don't think I can do this.'

Pebbles gave an encouraging bark. 'I believe in you, Fred,' he seemed to say. Or it might have been 'Pull yourself together' – Fred couldn't decide which.

That evening the Theatre Royal was packed with people. Everyone wanted to see their favourite street performer finally on the big stage. Fred had fixed his mask firmly to his face before he entered the theatre. The theatre curtains were lowered when Fred stepped on to the stage. It felt amazing to be there, though he could feel his legs trembling a little. Nervously, he peeped through the curtains. So many people! Up in a balcony he spied Pebbles perched on a seat next to Lady Pomplepuff, his tiny tail wagging in time to her flitting fan.

'This is it now,' Fred told himself. 'No going back.' The orchestra struck up.

The curtain slowly began to rise. 'It's him, the Dazzling Dancer of Theatre Royal – horah!'

Fred began to dance. All those nerves oddly helped as they added to his determination and gave him a bit of edge. Round and round and round he span on tip toe. The audience were delighted – how did he do it? No one knew but the boy had a gift, by golly that was true.

'Horah! Bravo! Brilliant!' Fred finished by flinging himself into an elaborate bow and received a standing ovation, which is to say that everyone stood up to clap.

'I can't believe it,' breathed Fred as the sound of applause rang in his ears. 'I've done it, I've done it! It's all gone so well!'

Swept up in his triumph, full of joy, Fred decided to give his audience one last bow. He bent down low with a final flourish and … smack! His mask fell from his face on to the floor. Fred blinked in horrified disbelief as it smashed into golden pieces in front of his eyes. And just like that, in a matter of seconds the night had gone from a success to a disaster. The worst had happened. What was he going to do now? There was really nothing he *could* do but rise from his bow. Slowly, with his heart in his mouth, Fred stood up. The sight that met him gave him chills. The audience's faces were full of confusion, the spell they had been under was well and truly broken. Fred's true identity was revealed and things could only go down hill from here. He felt miserable.

'It's that boy from the street!' someone piped up angrily. 'I've seen him outside the bakery, begging for scraps. What's he doing up there on the big stage?'

'He's not magic,' cried another, 'he's just a street boy!'

'Just a street boy,' the murmurs continued throughout the theatre. 'Just a street boy.'

There comes a time when the only story worth telling is the truth, and such a time had come for Fred. 'It's true,' he addressed them all. 'You're right. I'm just a street boy. My name is not the Dazzling Dancer of Theatre Royal. My name is Fred, just Fred, nothing else. I used to dance on the streets, though no one paid attention to me until I put on the mask. But no mask could hide who I really am inside. I've always been this person, the same person who only moments ago you found charming and entertaining. But now I feel ashamed to say who I am.'

Fred looked down at his feet. The theatre was silent. Then all of a sudden someone started to chant. 'One of us, one of us.'

Fred looked up to see that the people dressed in rags and tatters, just like him, were cheering and chanting 'One of us, one of us!'

'He's just Fred, nothing else and we love him for who he is,' someone cried. Then everyone in the theatre, the gentry too, began clapping and singing. 'He's just Fred, nothing else, just Fred, nothing else!'

Lady Pomplepuff rose gracefully from her seat in the balcony, Pebbles in her arms. Everyone fell silent to listen to this respected lady. 'This is a marvellous surprise, just Fred nothing else,' she said, 'but there is one question yet to be answered. Please tell us all … how did you get to be such a fantastic dancer? You're so talented, it can't be natural, it must be magic.'

'Thank you, most kind and elegant Lady Pomplepuff,' said Fred. 'But really, everyone is just as talented as me. You see, everyone has a gift, something special and unique about them, but a gift doesn't just become the best it could be without any work. The secret to my skills isn't magic. It's practice! Every day on the streets I practised and practised so that when my chance finally came, I was ready. That and, well … once I hear the music I just have to move!'

Then there was really nothing for it but to dance! The orchestra struck up and everyone in the theatre all danced together. After that day, Fred set up his own performance school for children who had faced the same difficulties in life as he had. Lady Pomplepuff gave them a space at her grand house where they could all stay. Together they helped the children to discover their gifts and get better with practice.

Pebbles discovered that he had a gift for chasing his tiny tail and practised running round and round until he could catch it. Rumour has it he's still practising to this day! Of course, Fred still performed at the Theatre Royal. He always wore a fancy mask for a bit of … *theatrical flair*. Audiences loved him. 'It's him, he's here!' With a rat-a-tat-ta-da! The Dazzling Dancer of Theatre Royal – horah!

He did it with practice; now everyone knew that the boy had a gift and by golly … so do you!

FABULOUS FOOTNOTES

Should you take a walk – or, indeed, a dance – along Theatre Street, you would see a modern version of Norwich Theatre Royal. You would also see the Assembly Rooms, a beautiful and welcoming building which still looks every bit as sumptuous as the cakes it offers, many of which I sampled for serious research purposes. As we discovered in the story, the Theatre Royal and Assembly Rooms were built by master builder Thomas Ivory in Georgian times; both were places of entertainment but the Assembly Rooms were reserved for the Georgian gentry. Thomas Ivory also built the Octagon Chapel which you can see in Colgate, Norwich. In 1768, Thomas Ivory was granted a licence for the theatre to become the Theatre Royal. The licence was granted by an Act of Parliament and given the royal assent. A group of the theatre's performers, called the Norwich Company of Comedians, then became known as His Majesty's Servants. In the archives at Norfolk Heritage Centre, I searched copies of *The Norfolk Chronicle* for theatre advertisements. Here I found a piece of writer's gold! The article featured in this story for *The Beggar's Opera* and *Wit's Last Stake* was written in the exact same year that I wanted to set the story, 1769, a time of Georgian extravagance. These were the landmarks and objects that inspired this imaginary story: ta-da! What sort of story would you make up about a Georgian theatre?

2

A BRUSH WITH SHOWBIZ FOR WILLAMINA WHISKERS OF WYMONDHAM

This rhyme is in a rush, a rush
To tell you about a brush, a brush
A brush with history on Wymondham streets
this story is going to sweep, to sweep!
It all begins with a mouse, a mouse
Who lives in a beautiful house, a house
A house that's tiny, sweet and sublime
And so it begins with *once upon a time* ...

Once upon a time there lived a little mouse called Willamina Whiskers, who was very neat and tidy. Willamina lived at No. 1 Flowerpot Cottage, the most beautifully kept crack in a flowerpot you ever did see. Inside she had a matchbox lined with feathers for a bed. There was a sturdy stick for a writing desk and a thimble for a chair. She had a patchwork rug made from bits and bobs of thread she had woven together. Her washing line was a piece of string with tiny pegs. Outside flowers swirled and drooped from the top of the flowerpot around the doorway. Willamina had made a door from a piece of wood with a knocker shaped like a mouse's nose. There was a door mat with the words *Welcome friend, please wipe your feet/claws/paws*. Willamina had written the letters herself using a blue crayon she'd found outside the library. The crayon also served well as a coat stand on which to hang all of her pretty hats and coats.

Willamina loved to sweep and her most precious possessions were brushes and brooms made from twigs. Sometimes she would sweep the whole street as well. Flowerpot Cottage sat merrily in the middle of Church Street in Wymondham opposite a lovely building called the Green Dragon, a tavern dating back to the fourteenth century with black and white beams and flowers at the windows.

The Green Dragon himself was a friendly creature who watched over the street and made sure that all the little animals living there were safe and happy. Willamina was surrounded by lots of friends: there was Bobby Button Nose, who lived at No. 2 Crack in the Pavement Close; Millie Mop Tail, who lived at No. 3 Twig Thistle Thatch; Johnny Jumpy Feet at No. 4 Hole in the Wall Way; Holly Hop Toes at No. 5 Rose Petal Pot. Further off in a field Sir Percy Pointy Ears the 67th lived at Tree Trunk Towers. This was a very grand home, with stretches of grassy land dotted with smaller tree stumps which also belonged to the Pointy Ears dynasty. Willamina adored her friends and went to visit them every day. She always took a brush with her in case they needed any help with sweeping and cleaning. Her friends were very grateful to have such a helpful and considerate mouse in the neighbourhood.

Now, after that rather peachy beginning it would be super if the rest of the story was about how everyone had a nice time. Unfortunately a bit of trouble was stirring. It all started when the Green Dragon flew off on holiday. He told everyone he would be back in a week but wanted to visit his friend Sir Jem Jolly Japers of Dragon Hall, Norwich. With no big green beast to protect the street, some mischief makers came out of the woodwork. Quite literally; they had been hiding in trees for some time.

One such such mischief maker set out to Flowerpot Cottage. Bad fortune was ready to knock on Willamina's door that day. Willamina had no idea, thinking it to be a normal Tuesday and time to put the bins out. She scurried to her door with her acorn recycling bin where she was met by the shadow of a very large mouse. As the shadow grew closer, Willamina saw a mouse with two enormous ears and a nose that pointed out so far, she wondered if he could ever see past the end of it. He wore a long coat with as many holes as it had buttons.

'Well, well, well, what a lovely home you have here.' said the mouse. He had rather a sharp, snarling voice. It gave Willamina the shivers.

'Very nice, very nice indeed,' he continued.

'Thanks!' said Willamina. 'Pleased you like it. I do my best.'

'Allow me to introduce myself,' said the mouse. 'My name is Henry Horatio Orlando Romeo Mercutio Monologue Montague Mouse. Just Henry will do. I'm new to this particular neighbourhood. Thought I'd call round and make myself known.'

Willamina popped the acorn recycling bin behind the door. She liked to be polite and welcoming to visitors and reached out a paw. 'Willamina Whiskers.'

'Nice to meet you, Willamoana.'

'*Willamina*,' she corrected him.

'Now listen, here, Willamary,' Henry continued 'I've got some rather exciting news for you. This home of yours, it's not going to be yours for much longer. I'm going to take ownership of it and transform it into a theatre.'

'I beg your pardon?' Willamina wondered if she'd been so busy cleaning out the piping that she'd forgotten to clean out her own ears.

'You heard,' said Henry. 'A theatre. Can't you just see it now, Willaminor?'

'*Willamina.*'

'Picture with me, Willamara,' Henry said and he waved his arms about. 'Over there, a stage for actors to perform.'

Gasp, went Willamina, my writing desk!

'Over there is where our audience will sit with snacks.'

Gasp, went Willamina, my patchwork rug!

'And that bit over there, I'm going to knock it down to make room for a second door. A stage door where actors can sign autographs, take selfies with fans and the like.'

Gasp, went Willamina, my poor cottage!

'We need Flowerpot Cottage, you see,' said Henry. 'There are no theatres for mice in the area and we decided that this was the prettiest place to have one. Good for tourism.'

'What do you mean *we*?' asked Willamina. 'What right do you have to do this? Are you important?'

Henry reached into his long coat and took out a badge. Gasp, went Willamina. It was the official seal of Mouse County Council.

'Important enough for you?' Henry asked.

Willamina was confused. Mouse County Council usually did such wonderful things for everyone. They had built community parks and gardens, introduced the great weekly plastic and recycling sweep up, they hosted street parties and offered apprenticeships to promising young musician mice, a chance to play lollipop sticks professionally. Forcing her to move out of her beloved home just didn't seem like the sort of thing they would do. There was something very suspicious about all this, very suspicious indeed.

'I'll give you three days to move out,' Henry said. 'Just call me generous. Pack up your bits and bobs and brooms and what-nots and be gone from here. After that, this place will be mine. I'm going make it into the greatest theatre the world has ever seen and then I'll be famous. I mean, this whole street will be famous. Tourists will flock to see me. I mean, us!' He laughed a sneaky laugh and with that he left.

'But that's not fair,' Willamina called after him.

'No,' said Henry. 'But hey, that's showbiz.'

As soon as Henry had disappeared from sight, Willamina burst into tears. But no, she wasn't going to let that mean mouse get the better of her. 'There must be a way,' she thought, 'a way I can keep my beautiful home. I know, I just have to make a theatre! A theatre that isn't at Flowerpot Cottage, a theatre that's good for the community and tourism. Then, if there already *is* a successful theatre, that horrible mouse will no longer have a reason to use my home. Yes, that's it! I can do this!'

Willamina scurried to her friends' houses to tell them what had happened. Everyone knew how much Willamina loved her home, and they were all very caring and wanted to help her make an amazing theatre.

'It seems to me,' said Sir Percy Pointy Ears, 'that our chosen location must be special. Willamina, I would like to offer up the grounds of Tree Trunk Towers. You've always been so kind with helping me to clean it, I must help you. That large stump over there will make an excellent stage for an outside theatre. It's big enough that should it rain, we can all go inside.'

'Hooray!' cried Willamina, 'That's perfect. Thank you, Sir Percy, what a gent you are!'

Now that the location for the theatre was sorted they needed to come up with a show.

'It needs to be something interesting and unusual,' said Willamina, 'something more than just mice performing on stage. That's what Henry had in mind, so we need a different idea.'

'What about a show that brings to life the history of the area?' suggested Bobby Button Nose. 'There used to be a brush factory in Wymondham, you know, on Lady's Lane, my late cousin Charlie Cheeky Feet used to visit. Willamina, you are well known for being kind and helpful with all your sweeping. I bet the mice would listen to you talk about brushes.'

'That's a brilliant idea,' said Willamina. 'I can see it now: *A Brush With History*. I bet those nice people at the Wymondham Heritage Museum can help us. Come on, let's go!'

The mice all dashed off to Wymondham Heritage Museum, where they discovered that Wymondham had a long history of wood turning and brush making.

'That town sign I pass every day on my way to Church Street has a picture of a wood turner on it,' said Willamina. 'I never knew that. Oh, and at the marketplace you can see carved spoons on the market cross to represent the craft of wood turning in the area.'

As if that wasn't enough to sweep them away, they found a whole room full of brushes.

Paintbrushes, shoebrushes, scrubbing and laundry brushes and the famous Besom Broom. The brush factory visited by Charlie Cheeky Feet was home of the Briton Brush Company.

'We can make some of these brushes for the show using twigs,' Willamina suggested. 'We may not have a factory but we do have friends, we can all help!'

Rehearsals at Tree Trunk Towers were in full swing. Willamina was busy practising on the tree stump when all of a sudden, a sharp, snarling voice snuck up behind her.

'I see what you're all doing, Willameya.'

Willamina turned to see Henry. She narrowed her eyes at him. 'Good, because we're putting on quite the show.'

Henry gritted his teeth, frustrated. 'Brushes?' He rolled back his head and laughed. 'Brushes? Do you honestly think that the trendy, super-cool mice of Wymondham are going to be interested in you talking about sweeping?'

A pang of nerves went straight to Willamina's tummy. He had a point. She was deeply worried that no one would turn up at all. But no, she couldn't let her doubts get the better of her.

'You'd better prepare for failure,' said Henry, 'because … because … you're going to fail!'

Willamina stayed calm. 'No,' she said. 'No, we are not going to fail. We've come up with a brilliant idea and worked hard as a team.' She couldn't quite believe her own confidence. 'The trendy, super-cool mice of Wymondham will be interested and supportive. In fact, this place is going to be packed. Our theatre will be a success. I'll get to keep my lovely Flowerpot Cottage.' With that she left him as he stood there, mouth open, gawping.

'But that's not fair!' Henry called after her.

'No,' said Willamina. 'But hey, that's showbiz.'

It was the day of the show, a sunny Friday afternoon, the third day Willamina was given to leave Flowerpot Cottage. She hadn't packed away any of her things. The theatre had to work, it just had to. Sure enough, mice flocked from all over Norfolk to watch the show. Rumour had spread of how hard Willamina's little theatre company had worked and how much she cared about cleaning in the community. The mice gathered on the grass; some set up rugs to sit on and enjoyed the picnics they brought with them. Willamina felt strangely confident as she walked on to stage.

'Ladies and Gentlemice, are you ready to get swept back in time?'

'Yes!' cried the mice. It was very encouraging to have such an excited audience and on Willamina went with the show. It finished to a hearty round of applause. Willamina felt wonderful until, all of a sudden, she heard the sound of slow clapping from behind her. The slow clapping grew closer as though creeping up on her.

'Very good Willamora, very good. You put on an excellent show,' came a sharp, snarling voice.

'He's behind you!' a mouse shouted from the audience.

Willamina turned to see Henry. Had he really just come up on stage to congratulate her?

'But I'm afraid that's not going to save you now.' Henry whirled around her. 'We're *still* taking your home. I will have my theatre!' He whipped a paw into his long coat and pulled out his badge. 'Your brush with success means nothing. Mouse County Council still has the power to take Flowerpot Cottage away.'

Gasp, went Willamina. Then she composed herself.

'Oh really? That's not going to happen and do you know why?' She took a deep breath. 'Because you're not from Mouse County Council.'

Gasp, went Henry.

Willamina reached out and pulled at Henry's long pointy nose. It came right off. Underneath was just a normal mouse nose, about average size.

Gasp, went the audience.

'You were just nosing around, you nosy so and so. I've had a funny feeling about you this whole time.' Willamina whirled around Henry.

'Ladies and Gentlemice, this mouse is an actor! I knew I recognised him from smelly cheese commercials. Henry, you don't have any power to take my home away. And besides,' she pointed into the audience, 'the Head of Mouse County Council is over there, eating snacks and enjoying herself. *You* Henry, wanted to take my home and make a theatre for yourself so that you could be famous. You dressed up and pretended to be from Mouse County Council when the truth is, they would never do such a mean thing.'

At that point, the Head of Mouse County Council stood up and called out, 'That's right, Willamina. We would never dress up and pretend to be ourselves in an attempt to take your home away.'

Henry burst into tears. 'You're right. I just wanted my own theatre, a place where I could finally perform to a real audience. Your beautiful Flowerpot Cottage was perfect, so well looked after and loved. But now my chance is ruined. I'll never get to show you all my Hamlet.'

'The shame of it is,' said Willamina, 'if only you had been nice and not tried to trick me,

we could have been friends. Then I would have helped you to perform. This theatre was built on friendship. When we all come together, look what we can achieve!'

'Friendship?' Henry rolled the word on his tongue as though trying it out for the first time. 'I'd never thought of that. Sounds good.'

'Well, it's not too late,' said Willamina. 'We could support you as an actor at our theatre. Provided you change your ways and never lie and pretend to be someone you're not ever again. Unless, of course, you are genuinely acting.'

'Yes please,' said Henry. 'I would love to be friends.'

Willamina reached out her paw and he took it.

'Thank you *Willamina.*'

At last, he had got her name right. 'Now, Henry,' smiled Willamina, 'your audience awaits. We are ready to watch you perform. These brushes make wonderful props and characters, you know.'

Full of excitement, Henry stepped into the spotlight. He gave them his Hamlet. 'To brush or not to brush?'

After that, the theatre at Tree Trunk Towers continued to thrive. *A Brush With History* was one of the most popular, in-demand shows as the trendy, super-cool mice of Wymondham were very interested in the heritage of the area.

The Green Dragon flew back from his holiday. He'd had a great time but home was the best place. He was delighted to find a new community theatre and enjoyed watching Henry's sell-out Shakespearean plays. *A Midsummer Night's Dream* was his favourite.

'I like how the brushes play all the trees in the fairy forest.'

As for Willamina Whiskers, well, she got to keep Flowerpot Cottage, she'd made new friends and developed a taste for the theatre. Perhaps best of all, however, was the thing that, deep down, she was most excited about. All these new brushes! Sweeping and cleaning would always be such fun. What a peachy ending for a very neat and tidy mouse.

FABULOUS FOOTNOTES

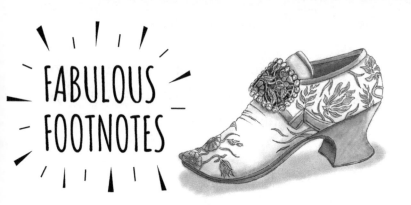

Should you visit Wymondham you too can get swept back in time. You can spot all the sights the mice would have seen, the Green Dragon on Church Street, the town sign with the picture of a wood turner, the market cross with carved spoons and spigots and indeed, Tree Trunk Towers. Well, you may not exactly be able to spy the residence of Sir Percy Pointy Ears but you can see the grounds in which it is set – Wymondham Abbey. This building dates all the way back to Norman times and was used by monks. At Wymondham Heritage Centre you can brush up on your history in the room filled with, you guessed it … brushes! Here I found a picture of the Brush Works on Lady's Lane.

If you were going to make up a show about the history of Wymondham, how would you sweep your audience away?

3

THE INGENIOUS INVENTOR OF DRAGON HALL

Dragons are mighty, magical things
Breathing fire and flying on wings
There are many myths and tales
of mischievous dragons with fiery scales
You may think there is nothing scarier
than a dragon in your local area!

In Norfolk dragons can be spotted
in museums, churches and buildings, dotted
with mystery, these majestic creatures
decorate lots of historical features.

At Norwich Castle of adventure,
in books at Norfolk Heritage Centre
are dragons from medieval days
they starred in street processions and plays.
'St George and the Dragon' told with imagination
marked the 23rd of April Guild Day celebration.
A crowd would gather outside Norwich Cathedral
to see a knight brave and a princess regal.
Now for the best moment – 'Everyone cheer and clap
for the arrival of our favourite dragon … Snap!'

This story, now you're in for a treat
is set on Norwich's King Street
where a medieval building we call Dragon Hall
houses the most spectacular dragon of all.
Let's step back to medieval days
to learn about the dragon's playful ways

Back then the streets were busy and rather smelly too
without proper toilets the air reeked of …
something whiffy!

The building, a splendid sight to knock off your socks
was created by a merchant called Robert Toppes
Toppes built a reputation which history cannot fade
A very busy merchant, successful in cloth trade.
King Street was close enough to the River Wensum
that boats could sale off to trade goods,
bring back more goods … and then some!

Now the scene is set, a great building near the water
Let us imagine the merchant had a daughter
A bright, ambitious, clever child
With a boisterous will, adventurous, wild!

The dragon and girl become best friends
You'll know how that happens once this story ends
Friendship born of imagination's prime
And so it begins with once upon a time …

Once upon a time there lived a great inventor. Her name was Margaret, Inventor Extraordinary, Out of the Ordinary, Doer, Maker, Mover, Shaker and all round Ground Breaker, Oh So Splendid, Terribly Clever, Greatest Inventor in the History of Ever! No, wait, that wasn't her real name, that was a name she invented for herself. You see, she was so good at making things up she's even managed to con-fuddle the narrator! Ahem, let's start again … Her name was Margaret Toppes, a little girl with big ideas. Margaret lived in a time called the Middle Ages. Back then, it was very different from how it is today. There were no cars or buses, so if you wanted to get somewhere you could ride a horse or walk on foot. Now all this walking might be exhausting but don't worry, Margaret has invented a new style of transporting yourself: Margaret's Merry Jolly Jumpy Springy Skippy Hop.

'Hop your way to a brighter day. Get places faster and with a creative flair! Thank me later. Margaret.'

There were no televisions or computers or phones: in fact, the digital screen was never seen! If you wanted entertainment, imagination was the order of the day and Margaret had plenty.

'Enjoy reading my epic stories of Peter the runaway pie. Long winter evenings need never be boring. You're welcome. Margaret.'

The streets were very dirty and smelly. But don't worry, Margaret has invented a very helpful 'nosy posy'.

'Protect your nose from yucky smells and nose on the neighbours at the same time! Stick the sticky stick to your forehead and dangle the sweet smelly dangly daisy in front of your face. As you walk along, the neighbours will think you look so funny, they will have no idea that you're spying on them! Have fun. Margaret.'

Margaret lived in a big house in the south Norfolk countryside with her family. All of her brothers and sisters grew up playing outside and climbing trees. Well, Margaret didn't climb trees as she was rather afraid of heights and her knees went wobbly. She was very fond of sitting under trees, however, to tell her tales of pesky pies to a happy group of listeners. Her most enthusiastic listener was her younger sister Anne, or 'Annie the Giggles', as Margaret called her. Margaret loved Anne to bits, her silly little sister full of giggles. Sometimes, only sometimes, she found it rather annoying when she had to look after Anne. If ever she tried to sneak away or hide from her big-sister responsibilities, soon enough she would hear Anne's giggles followed by 'Margaret, boo! I've found you!'

Margaret often wished that she could leave their south Norfolk home and stay with Dad in Norwich. Dad often worked and lived away from home; he worked in a very grand building with a great hall where he traded goods like cloth and spices. Margaret missed Dad a lot as she looked up to him and wanted to be just like him. She knew that Dad was a 'self-made' respected and successful merchant. These days we would call him an 'entrepreneur', meaning that he came up with ideas and worked very hard to put those ideas into action; he made his own way in the world. Margaret longed to see the great hall where Dad worked and he promised that he would show her round one day. Now, 'one day' seemed like a long time away, though soon enough it became tomorrow.

Mum told Margaret that they were going to travel to Norwich to visit Dad and no, they were not going to hop there! Margaret was over the moon with excitement.

'Finally, my chance to see Dad's great hall! And a great hall calls for a great invention, I can't wait to see what sort of ideas I come up with!'

When she got there at last, the building was even better than she expected. On King Street stood a grand door; Margaret felt sure it would lead to something magical. Inside the building, Dad walked Margaret through a screened passage and up some steps. Then they had to climb a very large staircase to get to the great hall. 'Wait for me, Margaret,' said Anne. Ah yes, Anne had insisted that she go with them. Margaret held Anne's hand to help her climb the staircase until, at last, they set foot in the great hall.

'I wanted the great hall to look, well … great!' explained Dad. 'Good impressions make for good sales. When people step inside this room I want them to feel a sense of splendour, magnificence, awe and majesty.'

'Ooo, yes,' said Margaret. 'It's all of those things, all at once, in that order.' She saw many tables draped with fine cloth and supposed that if she were a grown-up she would certainly buy one; a grown-up great inventor needs a grown-up great inventor's cape.

'Now look up,' Dad said. Margaret looked up to the ceiling, so high it made her feel dizzy.

'You see those beams above you,' said Dad, 'the triangle bit at each side of the arch is called a spandrel. There are lots of spandrels in this room, soom on one side, some on the other. And do you see what's carved in the middle of some spandrels on this side of the hall?'

'Dragons!' cried Margaret. The dragons were green with swirling wings and fiery red tongues.

'The dragons are made of baltic oak, good and strong,' explained Dad. 'You will see St George carved in the spandrels on the other side of the hall. I'm a member of the Guild of St George, you see, and so I thought the St George and the dragon story would go down a treat. Impressive, that's the look I'm going for and dragons do just the trick.'

'They would look even more impressive if they came to life,' thought Margaret. 'You couldn't not feel impressed with lots of live dragons flapping around your head. Might frighten a few folks away though,' she giggled, 'and the room would need to be even bigger for them all to whizz about in. Perhaps just the one dragon coming to life would be enough.'

Margaret skipped up to a dragon she best liked the look of. There was a certain charm about his grin. She had to stand on tiptoes to see him, way up above her.

'Now listen here,' she told him, 'my name is Margaret Toppes, I'm a great inventor just like my Dad. Hold still because I'm going to invent you.' Margaret rolled up the sleeves of her dress and stared at the dragon with determination.

'Your name is Sir Jem Jolly Japers. You can fly as high as the clouds in the sky. You like to eat cabbages because they make your fire go curly. And you can breathe smoke in different shapes like boats and trees and butterflies and flowers and … cabbages!'

No sooner had she said the word 'cabbages' than the dragon began to move, as though stirred awake by the mention of his favourite food. Magic sparks flew around him in all directions like little whizzes of lightning.

'Fizz, whizz, whoopeedoo and hello to you!'

Sir Jem Jolly Japers hovered in the air above her. He grinned a great big toothy grin and his tail whirled round and round, fast enough to make your head spin.

'Hooray!' cried Margaret. 'Look Anne, look what I did with my imagination. It's a real

live dragon. Can you see him cartwheeling through the air?'

Anne looked up and fell into heaps of giggles. 'He looks so silly!' she laughed.

'We're going to keep him and look after him,' said Margaret. 'His name is Sir Jem Jolly Japers.'

'Jem!' cried Anne.

'No,' Margaret rolled her eyes. 'Sir Jem Jolly Japers.'

But Anne was already running around the great hall with their dragon who gently blew little flower-shaped puffs of smoke as she chased him.

'Jem, Jem!'

'Oh all right then,' said Margaret. 'We'll call him Jem for short. But only, and I repeat *only*, because I say so.'

That afternoon the family were gathered round the table at Dad's house, chatting and eating. They ate meat pies, fish and vegetables. 'Look, Anne, can you see that curly little puff of smoke?' Margaret nudged her sister.

'It's coming from under the table.' The two peered under the table only to find …

'Fizz, whizz, whoopeedoo and hello to you!'

Jem sat with his long tail curled around him, merrily munching on a cabbage. He gulped down big mouthful then blew a tiny curly whirly puff of fire. 'Cabbages make my fire go curly!' he said. Margaret and Anne both fell into heaps of giggles.

'When can we take him out with us?' asked Anne.

'One day,' said Margaret. Now, 'one day' seemed like a long time away, though soon enough it became tomorrow.

It was spring and the family were staying at Dad's house in Norwich for the St George's Day celebration on 23 April. They were on their way to see the big procession outside Norwich Cathedral and the children were very excited. Margaret felt swept up in the buzz of it all, there were lots of people on the streets, all laughing and having a jolly time. Mum told Margaret to hold Anne's hand and not let her out of sight. But Margaret thought that was rather annoying; she wanted to go on ahead and see Norwich Cathedral in her own good pace. The closer they got to the cathedral the more crowded it became, Margaret could just make out the big pointy bits of the beautiful building in the distance. She could squeeze through the gaps between people to get a closer look if she just let go of Anne's hand.

'Wait for me, Margaret,' called Anne.

'No,' snapped Margaret. 'You can wait for me for a change. Stay there, I'm off to get a proper look at the cathedral without you.' With that she started to slip determinedly through the crowds of people by herself.

But the bustling crowds only seemed to get busier until Margaret realised that she hadn't got much further at all. What's more, she couldn't go back as she was wedged in the middle of a block of people. Margaret's eyes darted desperately around for Anne; she tried to spot where she had left her sister, only to find that one crowd of people looked much like another. 'It's all right,' she told herself, 'Anne is just over there. No wait, she's over there. Or is she over there? Or there? Oh, where did I leave Anne?'

Margaret's heart beat faster and faster in panic. 'Oh no, I should never have let go of Anne's hand.' She felt terrible, the worst she had ever felt. Tears prickled and her eyes went all blurry.

'Margaret, look up!' she heard a clear voice from high above her. It was Jem, sailing across the blue skies.

'No time for panic, Margaret,' he cried. 'You've got to find your sister. Now see, over there, a tree. If you climb up it you'll get a better view over the crowds. Follow me.'

Margaret followed Jem towards the tree, pushing and squeezing her way through the people.

'Oh no, but it's so high! I've never climbed trees, I've always been afraid of heights.'

'The time has come to conquer your fear,' said Jem. 'Quickly, get on with it.' Margaret got on with it and scrambled up the tree. She felt dizzy and her stomach wobbled, but she thought of how scared Anne must feel and carried on climbing. At last she reached a high branch where she got a clear view over the crowds.

'There she is! I see her!'

Poor Anne was crying and looked very lost. It was horrible to see 'Annie the Giggles' full of tears.

'Anne!' yelled Margaret. 'Stay there, I'm coming for you.'

Margaret jumped down from the tree and worked her way through the crowds until she had reached her sister. She flung her arms around Anne. 'Oh Anne, I'll never let go of you like that ever again, I promise.'

That night, in their shared bedroom, Margaret watched Anne sleeping peacefully in her bed.

'Fizz, whizz, whoopeedoo and hello to you!'

Jem whispered the words very softly as he appeared in their room.

'Jem!' Margaret ran up to her dragon and gave him a great big hug. 'Thank you for helping me find Anne today.'

'Well it was *you* who found her,' said Jem. 'You didn't need me.'

'I know,' said Margaret, 'but it was nice to have you there. I do love you Jem. You will always be here, won't you?'

'That I cannot promise,' said Jem.

'Why not?' Margaret asked.

'Because *you* won't always want me here,' said Jem. 'You see, I'm just the beginning of your many great inventions to come. Soon you will have busy, important things to do, big plans and even greater inventions to make. You won't want me getting in the way. When that time comes you will no longer be able to see me but you will know that I am certainly still there.'

Margaret was confused. 'But if I can't see you how will I know you are certainly still there?'

'Because there is no *certainly* as certain as the certainty that I love you and you love me,' said Jem. He flapped his wings playfully and span a little cartwheel in the air. 'It's that simple!'

'That doesn't sound simple to me,' said Margaret. 'I don't understand.'

'You will,' said Jem, 'one day.'

Now, 'one day' seemed like a long time away, though soon enough it became tomorrow.

A year passed and at the end of that year Margaret was a bit more grown-up. Just as Jem said, she was busy with important things to do, big plans and even greater inventions to make. Margaret relished having more responsibility and being entrusted with tasks. She was well on her way to becoming the ingenious inventor she dreamed she would be. At home in south Norfolk she scribbled stories, penned poems and mapped magnificent inventions including buildings with detailed descriptions of how to construct them. One day Margaret returned to Norwich with her family to visit Dad. She was allowed to visit the great hall again, but this time it was full of people come to buy goods. The people seemed very impressed by the great hall's grandeur; Margaret saw that Dad was making some smooth sales and wanted to help.

Meanwhile, Anne was running up and down the hall, full of giggles. 'Jem, Jem!'

'Who's Jem?' pondered Margaret. 'I remember that name, but I can't think who it is?'

'Jem is here!' Anne skipped up to her. 'Can you see him, Margaret? He's being very silly, spinning in the air and blowing smoke in the shape of boats. Up there!' Margaret looked up but all she could see was a beam with a spandrel. Inside the spandrel was a carved wooden dragon. A carved wooden dragon with a certain charm about his grin. 'Ah yes, of course, this was the dragon that I invented with my imagination.'

'Can you see him, Margaret?'

'Yes,' said Margaret. 'I can see him.'

It was true, she *could* see him. But not the cartwheeling, cabbage-loving Jem she had created. Just the carved wooden Jem in the spandrel. In that moment, Margaret finally understood what her lovely dragon had said to her a year ago. That he was just the beginning of her many great inventions to come and that even though she could no longer see him, she knew he was certainly still there. In her memories and her heart.

'Because there is no *certainly* as certain as the certainty that I love you and you love me.'

FABULOUS FOOTNOTES

In medieval days when people visited Robert Toppes's great hall to purchase goods, they might have travelled a long way to get there and would really take their time and make a day of it. This is why Robert Toppes made such an effort to make his great hall look splendid, so that the visit was an exciting event for people. Margaret would be fascinated to see the shops and cafes that line King Street today. There's a lovely sense of community on King Street and it's very interesting to see the mix of modern and medieval buildings. As well as the modern shops and community centres, you can see St Peter Parmentergate's Church dating to the fifteenth century. Dragon Hall is a beautiful building and inside you can see the great hall with its magnificent beams.

Dragon Hall is the home of the National Centre for Writing, a very creative and vibrant place that Margaret would have loved. One dragon remains in a spandrel, discovered during the late 1970s. Over the years changes had been made to the building and our dragon was hiding in an attic (built over the spandrel) – perhaps playing a very long game of hide and seek! Just imagine how it would have felt to make this discovery of a hidden dragon. This amazing find led to the building being known as Dragon Hall. In the Middle Ages, the Guild of St George used dragons as a symbol because of the story 'St George and the Dragon'. Perhaps this gave Robert Toppes the idea to decorate his great hall with dragons.

At Norfolk Heritage Centre I found old books with pictures of snapdragons. Snapdragons were used in the St George's Day celebrations that took place outside Norwich Cathedral during the fifteenth century. You can see snapdragons at the Museum of Norwich at the Bridewell and Norfolk Collections Centre, on site at Gressenhall Farm and Workhouse Museum. These are the landmarks and objects that inspired this imaginary story. How would you bring the dragon of Dragon Hall to life with your imagination?

4

SNUFFY AND THE STOLEN CUP OF QUEEN ELIZABETH I

This is the tale of a dog called Snuffy
Small and scruffy,
His eyes were sharp and his ears were fluffy
Nose on the scent, paws on track
Off on a quest for a cup to bring back.
Back in the time of Elizabethan history
Snuffy unravelled a Tudor mystery
Queen Elizabeth I made a progress
Through Norwich in a magnificent dress
Her progress had to be a success
And so Norwich gave her a gift to impress
A beautiful cup with coins inside

to mark this day of joy and pride
But before Her Majesty was given the gift ...
What's this? Oh no! The gift's gone adrift!
All of a sudden it was up to our pup
to find the queen's stolen gift of a cup
Then off went Snuffy, small and scruffy
His eyes were sharp and his ears were fluffy
Nose on the scent, paws on track,
He would find the queen's stolen cup
And bring it back!
Let us go then to the scene of the crime
And so it begins with once upon a time ...

Once upon a time, an Elizabethan time when Queen Elizabeth I ruled the land, Norwich received a spectacular royal visit. The queen graced Norwich with one of her famous street processions known as a progress. When word spread that she was coming, Norwich went up in arms with excitement. 'The queen's progress must be a success, she simply has to be impressed.' Merchants and nobles were excited, bakers and blacksmiths were delighted, but no one was as excited or delighted as a dog called Snuffy. Snuffy was Queen Elizabeth's biggest fan, he really thought she was the top dog. The queen, Snuffy thought, was the most marvellous monarch, both brave and kind because she had given permission for the Strangers to come to Norwich. The Strangers were talented weavers who came from overseas: Holland, Belgium and Luxembourg. Snuffy lived in a house which invited a group of Strangers to stay there and weave, we know this house as Strangers' Hall. No one in the house stayed a Stranger for long, however, and soon enough Snuffy had lots of new friends. He especially loved a girl called Beatrix and would often curl up with her next to the loom. The loom was a wooden object which held the threads together for weaving.

'You're my best friend in all the world,' Snuffy told Beatrix, though he knew that she could only hear him barking. Beatrix spoke Flemish, along with little bits of English she'd picked up, she sang songs and chatted to Snuffy about this and that. In this way, neither really understood what the other was saying but that didn't get in the way of friendship or stop them from being happy as can be in each other's company.

If it wasn't for Queen Elizabeth, Snuffy knew that the two would never have met and so he often imagined how he would thank Her Majesty should he have the honour of meeting her. Snuffy had heard all about the queen's fondness for dogs, and that she especially liked to see them in plays. William Shakespeare, Snuffy knew, often put dogs in his comedies on the big stage because it made the queen laugh to see them have fun. Snuffy dreamed that one day he could be in a great theatrical extravaganza where he was the dog to perform for the queen and make her smile. That really would be a nice way to say thank you. Now, when Snuffy found out that Queen Elizabeth was going to visit Norwich he was so elated that he ran round and round the garden, round and round again for good measure then pounced into Beatrix's arms for a big cuddle.

'Snuffy, I'm so excited too,' said Beatrix. She got a map and traced her finger along it to show Snuffy the route that the procession would take from St Stephen's Street to Bishop's Palace. Then Beatrix took a cup from the kitchen and explained to Snuffy, in the little English she knew, that the Strangers were going to present the queen with a magnificent cup containing coins as a gift. A cup, thought Snuffy, was a wonderful present; that way whenever the queen took a drink, she would be reminded of her lovely day in Norwich.

When the big day arrived, Snuffy and Beatrix joined the great crowd of people gathered outside St Stephen's Gate on St Stephen's Street. St Stephen's Gate wasn't just any old gate, you know. It was an enormous, grand gate with a stone arch; it was decorated with a Tudor rose, the white rose for the House of York and the red rose for the House of Lancaster, and so the Tudor rose was both white and red to show the two houses coming together. Near St Stephen's Gate a stage was set up with some looms and beautiful cloth woven by the Strangers to show Queen Elizabeth. Beatrix had helped to weave the cloth and so she was allowed to stand near it, Snuffy at her side. Beatrix had made a special little cloth handkerchief decorated with Tudor roses for Snuffy to wave as Queen Elizabeth passed by. Around them buzzed the excitement of chattering voices and the glorious smell of sweetmeats, fruit and all the yummy treats for special days. Then came music, loud and proud; 'ohhh,' went the crowd. Then came the mayor of Norwich looking very noble as he strode through St Stephen's Gate to lead the procession. 'Ahhh,' went the crowd. Then came the sight they had all been waiting for, Queen Elizabeth. 'Ohhh, ahhh, wow!' went the crowd. Everyone cheered and waved. 'Your Majesty! Your Majesty! Oh, doesn't she look fantastic?'

The queen rode gracefully on a horse. She wore a long, flowing dress of white and gold thread, covered with swirly patterns and pearls. Around her neck was a big sticky-out piece of stiff lace which Snuffy knew was called a ruff. The queen was surrounded by many nobles, following her nimbly, knobbly-kneed with nerves at the sight of their mighty monarch: nimble, nervous, knobbly-kneed nobles. Snuffy's eyes glistened to watch the elegant and powerful queen. He waved his little handkerchief. 'She really is the top dog!'

Queen Elizabeth graciously took her time to admire the beautiful woven cloth made by the Strangers. She congratulated them all on their skills and hard work – most kind of her to do so, thought Snuffy, as she must know how much her words mean to people. A thank you from the queen would go a long way in making everyone feel happy. It was wonderful to see Beatrix glow with pride; she deserved to be proud of her hard work. 'Thank you, Your Majesty' Beatrix curtseyed. 'And now, Your Majesty,' announced the mayor, 'the time has come to present you with your gift of a magnificent cup.'

Suddenly, a nervous knobbly-kneed noble nimbly ran up to the mayor and whispered something in his ear.

The mayor's face was a picture of confusion and worry. 'Missing, you say? Stolen!' he blurted out loud. 'I mean, yes yes, you're right, everything's going swimmingly well, absolutely to plan. Thank you, good fellow.'

Whispers of panic rippled through the close crowds who had heard the mayor's accidental outburst. People eyed each other suspiciously. 'Stolen? The cup's been stolen? How? By who? Don't you point at me!'

'Your Majesty,' stammered the mayor, trying to sound confident, 'we will present you with your gift at the end of the procession once we reach Bishop's Palace.' No one needed to say anything, Snuffy could see what everyone was thinking. *Oh dear, let's hope the cup turns up before then! Who's stolen it? How will we get it back?*

There was nothing to do but go on with the show. And on it went. On, on with the show! Everyone continued as normal. Everyone except Snuffy. Snuffy was very cross.

'Someone has stolen the queen's cup! That's not right at all. A gift for the queen is meant for the queen, not a thief.' An injustice had happened and he, Snuffy, was going to put wrong to right.

'Don't worry everyone,' Snuffy barked. 'I'll find Queen Elizabeth's stolen cup.' Then off went Snuffy, small and scruffy, his eyes were sharp and his ears were fluffy, nose on the scent, paws on track, he would find the queen's stolen cup and bring it back! Snuffy had memorised the route of the procession to the Bishop's Palace, which Beatrix had shown him on the map. A clever thief, he supposed, may well have memorised it too, that seemed like a clever thief sort of thing to do.

Snuffy charged along St Stephen's Street, weaving through people's feet, and on his way he spotted something twinkling in the corner of his eye. A golden coin, there next to a lady's foot. One of the golden coins from the cup. The thief must have dropped it. Snuffy picked up the coin and wrapped it in his handkerchief, carrying it to the marketplace at the end of St Stephen's Street. The marketplace was usually busy with the hustle and bustle of people but today all was quiet because most people were on St Stephen's Street watching the queen. Snuffy spotted another golden coin. The thief was leaving quite the accidental trail. He's not a very good thief, thought Snuffy. He picked up the coin and wrapped it in his handkerchief.

Then off went Snuffy, small and scruffy, his eyes were sharp and his ears were fluffy, nose on the scent, paws on track, he would find the queen's stolen cup and bring it back! Snuffy turned on to Dove Street where he spotted another golden coin, then he turned right on to St Andrew's Plain only to spot another. He picked up the coins and wrapped them in his handkerchief. Then off went Snuffy, small and scruffy, his eyes were sharp and his ears were fluffy, nose on the scent, paws on track, he would find the queen's stolen cup and bring it back! Along Prince's Street and across Tombland, more golden coins! This thief was doing a terrible job of not getting followed. Snuffy picked up the coins and wrapped them in his handkerchief.

Then off went Snuffy, small and scruffy, his eyes were sharp and his ears were fluffy, nose on the scent, paws on track, he would find the queen's stolen cup and bring it back! Finally he arrived at Bishop's Palace, and what do you think he saw? Queen Elizabeth's magnificent cup sat in broad daylight on the street. This was all very curious, thought Snuffy, what sort of thief leaves their stolen goods lying around for all to see? What with the trail of coins, it seemed almost as though the thief wanted the cup to be found. Still there was no time to think about it, he needed to get back to St Stephen's Street and the cup's rightful owner, Queen Elizabeth. Snuffy placed the handkerchief of coins securely inside the cup and put the cup carefully in his mouth. Then back went Snuffy, small and scruffy, his eyes were sharp and his ears were fluffy, nose on the scent, paws on track, he had found the queen's stolen cup, he would bring it back!

Snuffy charged on to St Stephen's Street and arrived to see Queen Elizabeth slowly making her way through on the horse. He put the cup down and barked with all his might. 'I've found it! I've found the Queen's stolen cup!' But of course, people didn't know what he was saying, they could only hear him barking. This really was too bad because had they understood him, the frenzy that followed would never have happened. People gathered around him angrily.

'Thief! Thief! He stole the queen's cup. Did you see, he had it in his mouth?'

'No!' Beatrix ran through the crowds and flung her arms around Snuffy. 'Snuffy's a good dog, a good dog!'

But her voiced was drowned out amid all the shouting. 'Thief! Thief! He stole the cup. And to walk around with it in his mouth like that, the nerve of it! Some dogs, eh?'

Poor Snuffy was very frightened. He had never considered that in finding the cup he would be accused of stealing it.

'Thief! Thief! Don't let him get away with it!'

Queen Elizabeth approached Snuffy. Her knobbly-kneed nervous nobles nimbly assisted her down from her horse.

'Oh dear,' squirmed Snuffy. This was it, his first encounter with the queen, the woman he looked up to and admired greatly and she thought he'd stolen her cup.

'Oh dear, oh dear, I'm going to get told off by Queen Elizabeth. And I didn't even do it!'

'Please, Your Majesty,' said Beatrix, 'Snuffy's a good dog.'

"Tis true!' a chirpy voice sang out from nowhere. Then all of a sudden, quicker than Snuffy could blink in confusion, a garish, colourful clown cartwheeled chaotically through the crowds and landed with a fanciful bow before Queen Elizabeth, bold as the morning sun.

'Your Majesty, 'tis I!' He announced himself as though he were quite the most important person ever to be seen on the street in spotty breeches.

'No need to introduce yourself,' said Queen Elizabeth. 'I know who you are. You are Will Kempe, famous actor and clown.'

Will Kempe giggled as though giddy with glee at the sound of his own name. 'Your Grace, 'twas I who stole your cup. Merrily I stole it for a joke, a jolly jest, a jovial jape! I thought it would be funny to sneak your gift away and leave a trail of coins to find it. What larks eh? But I couldn't let this little dog get the blame, that would never do. Faithfully, bravely this fine fluffy fellow embarked on a quest to find your cup. He's no thief. Look at him. Look at that fluffy face. He's so small and cute!'

'I'll give *you* small and cute!' growled Snuffy 'It's all very well playing tricks like that but stealing isn't funny. And neither are you. The nerve of it. Some actors eh?' Snuffy barked at Will Kempe like he meant business until he saw the queen stride towards him. Then all at once he came over very shy and nervous. What was she going to say?

The queen gave Snuffy a big kind smile. 'Be not afraid, little dog. You have done me a great justice this day. For your hard work and courage, thank you.'

Snuffy couldn't believe it. Her words of praise filled him with joy. What an honour to have such thanks from Queen Elizabeth.

Then the queen turned to Will Kempe. 'As for you! You're going to get a right royal telling off!'

Will Kempe fell at her feet. 'Your Majesty, I fall humbly at your feet. You see, Your Majesty, I'm in show business. I took a few dramatic liberties because I wanted to entertain you. Say you understand and I will dance a jig.'

'You are a very silly clown,' said Queen Elizabeth. 'Off with his head!' Will Kempe gasped. 'But Your Majesty, 'twas but a joke!'

Queen Elizabeth laughed. 'Now it is I who have played a joke on you. What larks, eh? I will pardon you because you were honest and came clean.'

Will Kempe very sincerely said he was sorry. Then he danced a jig. At the end of the procession, Will Kempe asked if he could put on a show to entertain everyone. Queen Elizabeth said yes, provided that he allowed Snuffy to be the star of the show. And so Snuffy's dream came true. He was the dog to perform for the queen and make her smile. A wonderful reward for putting wrong to right.

Later that day Snuffy went home with Beatrix. Both had been praised and thanked for their talents and hard work. Beatrix felt very encouraged to keep weaving the most wonderful cloth. As for Snuffy, he was as loyal and devoted to Queen Elizabeth as ever. He vowed that he would always be there to put wrong to right because her words of thanks had meant so much. After all, Snuffy would tell you, nothing beats a bit of appreciation from the top dog.

Hear ye, hear ye, a disclaimer! Will Kempe did not steal Queen Elizabeth I's cup.

FABULOUS FOOTNOTES

This story features two famous historical figures from Tudor times, Queen Elizabeth I and Will Kempe. The queen visited Norwich in 1578 with a procession of great pomp and theatricality. The street procession was, in a sense, a show for the people and the queen played the role of the elegant and powerful monarch that the working folk of Norwich wanted to see. For many people, this was their once-in-a-lifetime chance to see the queen, so the day would have been a real treat. She entered through St Stephen's Gate to excited Norwich crowds. She was greeted by the mayor of Norwich, admired the Strangers' weaving and was presented with a cup and coins as a gift. The gift was not stolen and Will Kempe did not meet the queen that day, that part was made up for the story. Much like Will Kempe, I took a few dramatic liberties because I wanted to entertain you.

Will Kempe, actor and clown, famously morris danced from London to Norwich and entered through St Stephen's Gate. Actors were often known as rogues and vagabonds and cheeky Will Kempe was no exception. Queen Elizabeth was a big fan of the theatre and so it seemed a fun idea to bring the two characters together for this story.

Now that you have read about St Stephen's Street, imagine what people from Tudor times would make of the street these days. It is just as busy and lively as it was back then, but with some very different places: shops, supermarkets and bus stops. St Stephen's Gate is no longer there and in its place is a roundabout, busy with traffic. Now, here's a sight for spotting – near the roundabout stands a pub called the Coachmakers Arms. On the outside of this pub is a big picture of St Stephen's Gate as it would have been.

These are the landmarks and objects that inspired this imaginary story.

Should you enter St Stephen's Street via the roundabout on a bus, just think that you are following in the footsteps of Queen Elizabeth I. Isn't that something!

5

GALLOPERS GO! THE MERRY-GO-RACE OF KING'S LYNN

Gallopers go, gallopers race
Gallopers fly at a galloping pace
Faster than a firework zooms
Faster than a lightning bolt
Faster than a spring bud blooms
Faster than a catapult
Gallopers run, gallopers chase
Gallopers go on a galloping race
A race through the history of King's Lynn
Which galloping galloper's going to win?

Galloping fun of fairground design
And so it begins with once upon a time ...

Once upon a midnight at Lynn Museum the fairground animals came to life. First Henrietta Horse leapt off the roundabout. 'Wheee, what fun!' She shook her beautiful silky mane. The museum was dark, though Henrietta sensed that during the day it was a vibrant, lively place. The air was riddled with mystery and, casting her eyes around the objects, she had that nice *no one's around, it's just me* sort of feeling. The roundabout stood at the entrance to the room, bursting with bright rainbow colours of red, blue, green and yellow; it looked ready for some serious fairground fun. Henrietta knew it was a model and much smaller than a real roundabout would have been. The model roundabout was called 'Fred Fox's Galloping Steam Horses'.

'That's me,' thought Henrietta, 'I'm a galloper!'

Powered by steam, such roundabouts often had other animals besides horses which you could ride on, like cockerels and peacocks, round and round at a gentle pace. Gentle, that is, until the animals came to life by magic at midnight. Then they could go really fast. None as fast as Henrietta. Faster than a firework zooms, faster than a lightning bolt, faster than a spring bud blooms, faster than a catapult, Henrietta was the fastest galloper *ever.* You could just make out her bright red saddle whizzing by like a fiery flare. *Whoosh!*

'Wowee,' said Henrietta. 'I wonder if I'm the only one tonight to ...'

'Hello Henrietta!' Zack jumped off the roundabout. He was a grand horse with a blue saddle and painted across his body were marvellous leaves of red and gold.

'Wowee,' said Henrietta, 'I wonder if we're the only ones to ...'

'Hello Henrietta!' Zara jumped off the roundabout. She was a lovely horse with a yellow and blue saddle. In her mane glistened a bright painted star.

'Wowee,' said Henrietta 'I wonder if we're the only ones to …'

'Hello Henrietta!' It was Ricky the Racing Cockerel. He was tall and graceful with grey feathers. His beak looked rather stern, though everyone knew him to be friendly.

'Wowee,' said Henrietta 'I'm guessing we're not the only ones to …'

'Hello Henrietta!' Jenny the Jumping Cat jumped off the roundabout. She cartwheeled round and round, her ginger stripes whirring like a spinning top.

'OK,' said Henrietta. 'I wonder who else will …'

'Greetings to you Henrietta!' Ronald the Racing Peacock glided elegantly off the roundabout. He was a somewhat superior creature with feathers of deepest blue, red, gold and green. Henrietta wasn't the biggest fan of Ronald. He had a rather pompous manner and could talk endlessly about himself. At heart, however, she knew him to be kind and, if you caught him in the right mood, funny. By this point all the other horses had jumped off the roundabout. They chatted excitedly about what they would do with their night. As they talked, Henrietta began to trot through the displays, looking for ideas. She saw all sorts of objects from the Iron Age to the Middle Ages, and from maritime history.

Then Henrietta saw a wooden carved dobby horse beautifully kept in a glass case. She read that the dobby horse was made in Victorian times by the Savage family of King's Lynn, the very same Savages who had made her. Henrietta knew that the Savages all started with Frederick Savage, an engineer with a big imagination. He started making machines for agriculture and went on to make fairground rides. The lovely little dobby horse was made for his children and went on to be used as a rocking horse by his grandchildren. The dobby horse had big glass eyes and his head tilted slightly to the left, as was the tradition with Savage's horses. Frederick Savage wasn't the only person to make roundabouts, but he certainly added his own creative twist to them, which made for very popular entertainment.

'Wowee,' said Henrietta, 'so much exciting history! Listen, everyone, I've got an idea. Looking round this museum has made me think what fun it would be to play a game. It could be a race, a merry-go-race through the history of King's Lynn. Everyone choose a street then we'll all go galloping and find out interesting things about the area. There needs to be at least one unusual discovery, something that you didn't know before. A *wild card* category, if you will. Whoever comes back the fastest, wins!'

'That sounds great,' said Jenny, and she somersaulted through the air. 'What will the prize be for the winner?'

'The winner gets to choose which part of history they found the most interesting and make up a story about it for everyone to listen to another midnight,' said Henrietta. 'Although we all win really. Everyone will have learned something amazing. The game is only meant to be a bit of fun.'

Ronald gave a cough: 'Ahem.' He always coughed before he spoke, as though he was about to say something of the utmost importance, even if it was only about biscuits. 'It's not that I don't like games,' he said, 'in the spirit of healthy competition and what have you. It's just that I have been known to win. I fear there would be no point in anyone else playing.'

'Oh, come off it, Ronald,' laughed Zack. 'If anyone's going to win it will be Henrietta. She's the fastest galloper there is, everyone knows that. Unstoppable!'

Henrietta looked down at her hooves and blushed. She couldn't help but feel rather proud of being the fastest ever. Someone had to be and, well, she did practise very hard. 'Thank you, Zack,' she said. 'I could give you all a head start if that's helpful?'

'Yes,' said Zack, 'I think a head start would be a nice thing to do. Otherwise there wouldn't be much point in us joining in. Right, let's play!'

'Now hold on to your horses.' Ronald chuckled at his own joke while everyone groaned. 'I'm eager to play – provided, that is, provided that awful flying pig doesn't join us. Still, I see no sign of him so one hopes for the best.'

At that moment Henrietta spied Frankie the Flying Pig wriggle his way off the roundabout. He trotted slowly and merrily towards Ronald.

'Erm, Ronald…'

'What's his name?' Ronald continued unaware. 'Danny or Frankie or something? Can't stand him. He thinks he's so …'

'Ronald …'

'Amusing. Well he's not. Irritating, more like. I shan't play if …'

'*Ronald*!'

Ronald ruffled his feathers, annoyed at being interrupted. 'I say, what?'

'Hello mate,' said a voice from behind him.

Ronald's eyes bulged with alarm and he slowly turned. 'Frankie! Oh, how do you do? I was just talking about how splendid it would be if you were to join us in our game.'

'How nice of you,' smiled Frankie. 'I'd be delighted to join your game and I would especially just love to be on *your* team, Ronald.'

'Henrietta, I'm afraid I can no longer play,' Ronald suddenly announced. 'I've just this instant come over unwell, sorry.'

'Don't be silly,' said Henrietta. 'And yes, teamwork is an excellent idea. Everybody find a partner, Ronald and Frankie pair up, Zack and Zara pair up, Ricky and Jenny pair up, all you horses pair up, that's right, now that just leaves … me!'

'Oh dear,' said Zara. 'Henrietta, you don't have a partner, I feel bad.'

'Now don't you fuss over me,' said Henrietta. 'It's no problem. This whole thing was my idea anyway. Now come on everyone, let's play. I'll count to ten merry-go-rounds to give you a heard start. Ready … steady … gallopers go!'

In a flash all the fairground animals sped out of the museum and on to the streets of King's Lynn. *Whoosh*! Henrietta stayed behind 'one merry-go-round, two merry-go-rounds, three merry-go-rounds …' As she counted she caught sight of something curious in the corner of her eye. Something moved, though she didn't see what it was and when she looked around everything was just as before. Then it moved again. Henrietta jumped. Something or someone was hiding in the shadows, watching her. 'Four merry-go-rounds, five merry-go-rounds, six merry-go-rounds ...' It couldn't have been any of the fairground animals, because she had just watched them all rush off onto the streets. Whatever was it? 'Seven merry go-rounds, eight merry-go-rounds, nine merry-go-rounds ...' Did it move again, quick as a blink? Or was she just imagining things? There was no time to wait and find out. 'Ten merry-go-rounds ...' Henrietta shot off on to the streets of King's Lynn.

Whoosh! Faster than a firework zooms, faster than a lightning bolt, faster than a spring bud blooms, faster than a catapult, Henrietta was the fastest galloper *ever*. She arrived on Purfleet Quay, her chosen spot for the game. King's Lynn, she knew, had a long history of fishing because it was so close to the sea and lots of fisherfolk would have lived and worked in the area, including on North

Street and Bridge Street. Henrietta had come to the quay as she wanted to see the statue of a sea captain that she'd often been told about. The sea captain wore a coat and hat with a scrolled map in his hand, looking out to sea as though he had spotted an interesting discovery far off in the distance. Henrietta read that the statue was of George Vancouver, born in King's Lynn in 1757. George Vancouver was an explorer, he went on sea voyages and helped to discover and make maps of the coast of North-West America.

'Well, there's something I never knew,' said Henrietta. 'Now, back to the museum.' She was about to take off when, all of a sudden, out of the corner of her eye, she saw it again! The curious, hiding thing. Whatever it was, it had followed her all the way to the quay. Henrietta looked around her only to see … nothing was there! Well, the statue was there. But it couldn't have been the statue that moved, could it?

'Is anyone here?' Henrietta called. No answer. Well, there was nothing for it but to get back to the museum. *Whoosh*! Henrietta arrived back to find she was the only one there. Or was she? Had the curious, hiding thing followed her back? Henrietta eyed the museum carefully. Everything was quiet. Then all of a sudden … *whoosh*! Zack and Zara arrived back. 'Uh oh,' laughed Zack. 'Looks like Henrietta's won even though she gave us a head start.'

Whoosh! Ricky and Jenny arrived back. 'That was so much fun!' Jenny flipped through the air and swished her tail. *Whoosh!* All the other horses began to arrive back. Everyone chatted excitedly about the history they had discovered.

'I think that's everyone back,' said Henrietta.

'Nope,' said Zack. 'We're waiting for Ronald and Frankie – let's hope they didn't get on each other's nerves.'

Whoosh! 'Oh I say, my good fellow, that really was most amusing,' Ronald was chirping with laughter, a wing wrapped around Frankie.

'Good to see you both,' said Henrietta, 'though I'm afraid you've arrived back last.'

'Oh, no matter,' said Ronald. 'We got chatting and this one had me in stitches, he's quite the comedian.'

'Here all week, ladies and gents,' smiled Frankie.

'Who won, by the way?' Ronald asked.

'Henrietta did,' said Zack. 'Fastest by far.'

Henrietta looked down at her hooves and blushed.

'Don't be embarrassed by your success,' said Zara. 'You won and well deserved. Congratulations.'

'Thank you,' said Henrietta. She told them all about the statue on the quay. 'Would anyone else like to share what they learned?'

'We would!' said Jenny, whirling around with glee. 'Ricky and I, we found out more about the Savages of King's Lynn. We went to the marketplace, once known as the Mart. Now, as we all know, in Victorian times, Frederick Savage made machines for agriculture then he turned his attention to making us – fabulous fairground animals! He also set up cottages for his workers to live in on George Street. He took his roundabouts to the Mart from his factory, St Nicholas Ironworks. I bet people had never seen gallopers like us before, no wonder we were so popular!'

'Frederick Savage made other rides,' continued Ricky. 'Including switchbacks. Big boats or fancy seats called gondolas went round and round on a track. Oh, and here's something for the wild card category – did you know that a lot of these rides could be made to order? The Savages had a catalogue, that's a book which showcased all their work and people could choose what to buy. The book was called *Roundabouts. Savage Brothers Ltd. St Nicholas Works. Kings Lynn-Eng–* Fancy that, Ronald, someone could have ordered a roundabout with more peacocks … more Ronalds!'

'I could be made to order!' Ronald gave an outburst, shocked at the notion that he might not be one of a kind.

'Don't worry,' said Ricky, 'the book said that orders would be *finished and decorated in our very best style.*'

Ronald raised an eyebrow. 'We'd better be.'

'Us next,' said Zack. 'Zara and I went to Queen Street. On Queen Street you can see Clifton House, dating from medieval times, and in the eighteenth century a rich merchant lived there.'

'And here's something for the wild card category,' said Zara. 'The front door has columns standing outside of it with lots of beautiful swirly patterns. They are now known as barley-sugar columns. Can you believe that's what they call the columns? Rather a delicious name, barley-sugar.'

'Yes,' said Frankie, 'I can *barley* believe it.' Everyone groaned.

'Now, time to tell you about King Street,' said Frankie. At this point Ronald began to hop up and down urgently. 'Oh please, oh please, let me tell them!'

Frankie smiled and continued. 'On King Street you can see the Guildhall of St George.

A beautiful building, built in the fifteenth century, that's medieval times. It's the largest surviving guildhall in England.'

'Oh please, oh please, I simply must tell them!' Ronald was about to burst. 'Today,' said Frankie, 'it's sometimes used as a theatre and, oh go on then Ronald, tell them. Here's something for the wild card category.'

Ronald gulped a great breath and took gallant strides forward as he spoke. 'Once more unto the breach, dear friends, once more.'

'I believe,' sighed Frankie, 'that my friend here would like you to guess which famous historical person he is quoting.'

Ronald stretched his wings out dramatically, 'Romeo, Romeo, wherefore art thou Romeo?'

Frankie rolled his eyes, 'All we can do is just let him have his moment.'

Ronald twirled around daintily. 'Shall I compare thee to a summer's day?'

'Who, me?' said Frankie. 'Please don't.'

Ronald thrust himself forward. 'To be or not to be?'

'I've got it,' cried Henrietta. 'I've read all about this. Ronald is quoting well-known lines from William Shakespeare. You know, the Tudor playwright. He's quoted *Henry V*, *Romeo and Juliet*, Sonnet 18 and *Hamlet*.

'Nice one, Henrietta,' said Frankie, 'all that reading you do pays off. Yes, there is evidence to suggest that Shakespeare himself played at the Guildhall of St George in the early 1590s, touring with the Earl of Pembroke's Players.'

Ronald collapsed to the floor in theatrical repose.

The fairground animals applauded him heartily.

'No, don't applaud him,' said Frankie. 'You'll only encourage …'

Suddenly Henrietta spied faint sunlight filtering through the window of the museum. 'Looks like daylight is coming,' she said, 'nearly time to go back to the roundabout, else the museum will open and the visitors will get a surprise!'

And right then, there in the shadows, she saw it again! The curious, hiding thing.

Henrietta had lost all patience by this point. 'Come out of there at once,' she called. 'I can see you and I know you're following me. Whatever you are come out and show yourself.' All the animals gaped at where Henrietta was staring. Together they saw a shy little head poke out from behind a display. The head tilted slightly to the left and had big glass eyes, blinking bashfully.

'I know who that is!' said Henrietta. 'It's … it's … Dobby Horse!'

'Dobby Horse!' cried everyone.

'Is this a dobby horse I see before me?' asked Ronald. Frankie rolled his eyes.

'I'm so sorry to bother you,' Dobby Horse said in a hushed, nervous voice.

'Oh, little Dobby Horse, it's all right,' said Henrietta, 'come out and join us.'

Quietly, cautiously, Dobby Horse shuffled towards the group. 'I didn't want to cause any trouble,' he mumbled, 'only I came to life while you were talking. I'm not from the roundabout and I felt like I didn't fit in so I hid and listened. Your game sounded really fun and I wanted to join in but I was too shy to ask.' He looked down at his hooves. 'I know I don't really fit in with you but I just wanted to play so I followed you to the quay and back. I'm so sorry if I caused any bother but it was nice to learn about the history of King's Lynn and to see that you won, Henrietta.'

'You mean we won,' said Henrietta.

Dobby Horse looked confused. 'We did?'

'Of course,' said Henrietta. 'We won. We were playing as a pair, didn't you know? You were my partner.'

'I was?'

'Well of course you were. We did this together. I think we made a great team.'

'We did?' Dobby Horse looked up from his hooves. 'Oh, that's brilliant.'

'Hooray!' cried everyone. 'Congratulations, Henrietta and Dobby Horse. What a pair of champions.'

'And remember you're welcome to join us any time,' said Henrietta. 'We love making new friends. Just join in next time us fairground animals come to life.'

Frankie gave a whistle. 'Fairground animals coming to life, eh? A likely story. Pigs will fly!'

Ronald rolled his eyes. 'Oh, for goodness' sake, how long have you been waiting to say that?'

'Too long,' said Frankie. 'It took me till the end of this story but I've finally said it.'

'Right, come on everyone, back to the roundabout,' said Henrietta. 'Until another midnight, Dobby Horse, see you then.' Dobby Horse climbed back into his glass case and settled comfortably. The animals all jumped back to their places on the roundabout. Only then did Henrietta realise that she hadn't claimed her prize, to choose which part of history she found most interesting and make up a story about it. No matter. It struck her that since they had talked about the Savage fairground animals, she herself was part of a story. And so she would give her prize to the person reading or listening to her story.

What did you find the most interesting? Which part of King's Lynn history would you like to make up a story about?

As the sun shone in through the window of the museum and the doors opened to welcome visitors, no one could have guessed what had happened that night. The fairground animals were all as still as statues. Until another midnight.

FABULOUS FOOTNOTES

It made perfect sense to set this story at King's Lynn Museum where you can see the model roundabout 'Fred Fox's Galloping Steam Horses'. Spot Henrietta with her red saddle! You can also see the lovely little dobby horse in his glass case. At Norfolk Heritage Centre, I found the very catalogue which Ricky the Racing Cockerel talks about where fairground rides and animals could be ordered: *Roundabouts, Savage Brothers Ltd, St Nicholas Works and Kings Lynn-Eng.* It's a bright yellow book with pictures and descriptions of many designs for entertainment known as 'novelties'. Such novelties include musical organs, steam swings, tandem bicycles, 'sea on land' (boats that go round and round on a track), roundabouts and fairground animals.

People could order from the catalogue using a telegraphic code (a bit like a phone, a telegraph was used when two people wanted to communicate over a long distance. They used electronic codes to send messages to each other). If you wanted to telegraph an order to be shipped in six weeks you would use the code word 'Novelle'. Just think how things have changed – these days we may choose to order items online with the simple click of a button! In King's Lynn, you can see all the sights mentioned in this story, the statue of George Vancouver on Purfleet Quay; the Mart, which is now a modern marketplace; Clifton House on Queen's Street, complete with barley-sugar columns; and St George's Guildhall on King Street, which is sometimes used as a theatre. These are the landmarks and objects which inspired this imaginary story. Would you like to claim Henrietta's prize and make up your own story inspired by King's Lynn history? Storytellers go!

6

THE AMAZING IMAGINARY ALPHABET CIRCUS OF GREAT YARMOUTH

Roll up, roll up for a circus spectacular!
Feast your eyes on the bedazzling
sight of Victoria Clown performing
her great tightrope walk, right here at
this fantastical venue, the Hippodrome.
Victoria Clown takes her place way up high,
high enough to touch the sky, balancing
on the tip of her toes, there she goes!

To see this marvellous circus we need to step back to Edwardian times when King Edward VII sat on the throne. On St George's Road, facing the sea, there stood the Hippodrome, a magnificent building for circus shows. This exciting venue for popular entertainment looked a treat as it was decorated with lots of swirling patterns and pictures of birds, all in a very decorative and elegant style called Art Nouveau. Inside the building, there was a big round stage known as 'the ring'. This ring was swimmingly good in more ways than one because it could transform into a water spectacle. The floor of the ring could lower using mechanics to reveal a big pool of water for an exciting splashing finale.

A little distance off along a row of houses sat No. 12; inside No. 12 sat the nursery, and inside the nursery sat Victoria. Well, she wasn't sitting, she was playing! Her nursery may not have been the real deal Hippodrome but she had put her imagination to good use, making it every bit as magical. The toys sat neatly in a circle around the ring in which Victoria performed. The toy fairground horses, tiny dolls from the doll's house, the rocking horse, George Teddybear, Daisy Doll, Laura Lion and the Punch and Judy puppets sat on the edge of their seats, spellbound as Victoria stepped on to the tightrope. The tightrope was a skipping rope stretched across the floor and Victoria, pretending it was up in the air, walked across it with terrific poise. Wibble, wobble, will she make it to the other end? Over Victoria's shoulder was a little umbrella; she had often seen clowns have one and it looked rather fancy. And of course, for some real theatrical flair Victoria had learned how to juggle. Hours of endless practice meant that she could now juggle soft balls in the air with great ease. As for the water spectacle, a blue rug on the floor made for a convincing pool of water, ready for Victoria Clown to make a splash.

'Isn't Victoria Clown wonderful?' The charmed audience clapped and cheered.

But one toy did not look as impressed as the others, and that toy was Edward Elephant.

He flapped his ears and swished his trunk. 'Victoria, you're supposed to take time today to practise your alphabet, remember? Nanny said.'

'Oh, but I'm too busy playing circus, can't you see?' said Victoria. 'I've learned all about the circus, you know. Nanny and I went on a walk yesterday along St George's Road and guess what we saw? The Hippodrome! Nanny read to me from a book that the Hippodrome was built for the great showman, George Gilbert.'

'That's very interesting,' said Edward Elephant. 'Just think, once you've learned your alphabet, in time you will be able to read your own books and learn more exciting things about the circus.'

But Victoria wasn't paying attention. She was too busy pretending to be a tumbler. She tumbled to the ground, did a roly-poly and shot up on her feet into an outburst of energetic star jumps.

'I've got an idea,' said Edward Elephant. 'Let's make our very own imaginary circus using the alphabet. Why not include some of our toy friends here? I'm sure they would love to play.'

Victoria skipped in a circle around Edward Elephant. 'Look, I'm an acrobat.'

'Great start,' said Edward Elephant. 'A is for acrobat. We can certainly have lots of acrobats in our circus. Now what could we have beginning with B?'

'What about bicycles?' said Victoria. 'I've seen people ride bicycles that look like a tricky circus trick. Those ones I'm thinking of have a great big front wheel and a very small back wheel.'

'Ah yes,' said Edward Elephant. 'I think the bicycles you mean are called penny-farthings. They do look rather tricky to ride don't they? I'm sure George Teddybear would like to try his hand – or, rather, his paw – at riding a penny-farthing for the circus performance. Now, what about C?'

'That's easy,' said Victoria, 'clowns. Look, I'm Victoria Clown.'

'The star of the show,' smiled Edward Elephant. 'Now, how could Daisy Doll and all our tiny dolls here join in? Something beginning with D?'

'Dancers!' said Victoria. 'I think the dolls would love to dance.'

'Excellent idea,' said Edward Elephant. 'We've got rather a fun alphabet circus going here.'

A is for Acrobats, swinging in the air.
B is for Bicycles, busy whizzing teddy bear.
C is for Clowns, performing harlequins.
D is for Dancers, see how Daisy Doll spins!
E is for …

Edward Elephant went quiet. 'Well, Victoria, what does E stand for?'

'Oh, I just don't know,' said Victoria. Edward Elephant's trunk drooped down shyly.

'Of course I know!' Victoria ran up to him and gave him a hug. 'You! We've got to have *you* in the circus.'

Edward Elephant flapped his ears and swished his trunk. 'Well, we wouldn't want real animals in a show. But we could have toy and imaginary animals like me. What could I do?'

'Hmmm,' said Victoria. 'I think that Edward Elephant could ... stay quiet. That can be your circus trick.'

'Now, why should I stay quiet?' asked Edward Elephant. 'I sense some mischief is at work here.'

'Not at all,' said Victoria. 'Nanny said that some E's are silent. So you would be a silent E.'

'Only some E's are silent,' said Edward Elephant. 'The ones that go at the end of words like *make* and *bake* and *cake*. The E that goes at the front of words like Edward and elephant are loud. That means I can make as much noise as I want.' He shot his trunk into the air and gave a vigorous trumpet call which left Victoria in heaps of giggles.

'Now, Victoria, you're getting good at this,' said Edward Elephant. 'Let's see if we can really get these letters swinging and make our imaginary circus come to life. Let's go!'

F is for Fairground animals, horses leap and glide.

G is for Games, hopscotch and helter-skelter ride.

H is for Hippodrome, our Great Yarmouth venue.

I is for Ice cream, yummy treats on the menu.

J is for Jugglers, spinning balls round and round.

K is for King Edward, let's make the royalty proud.

L is for Laura Lion, she joins in with a grrrrrrrrr.

M is for Masks, masked dancers whizz and whirrrrrrrr.

N is for Nautical, singing sailors, seaside sand.

O is for Orchestra, strike up the band!

P is for Punch and Judy, *that's the way we do it.*

Q is for Queue, there's a queue to get in, I knew it!

'I think a queue can be a very good thing,' said Edward Elephant. 'It creates a sense of anticipation and buzz before the show.'

'True,' said Victoria. 'Nanny once said that no respectable entertainment attraction is complete without a ridiculously long queue to get in. Now, where were we? Ah yes, time for the rocking horse to join in.'

R is for Rocking Horse, swaying to and fro.
S is for Swimmers, splash, there they go!

'Swimmers, Victoria?' Edward Elephant was curious.

'Yes,' said Victoria. 'The Hippodrome has an inside water spectacle for swimmingly good performances, and so do we, look!' She pointed to the blue rug.

'Ah, of course,' said Edward Elephant. 'How did I not see? Now where were we … T.'

T is for Tightrope, wibble, wobble, stay on top.
U is for Umbrella, a clown's fancy prop.

V is for Victoria, the star of the show.
W is for Water Spectacle, let it ripple and
flow.
X is for … X is for … X is for …

'Oh dear,' said Victoria. 'I can't think of
anything.'

'Yes, that's a tricky one,' said Edward
Elephant. 'Perhaps, given the playful nature
of our imaginary circus, our beloved audience
might permit us to do a bit of a cheat. We
could use the sound of X to create the words.
For example, we could say that our circus is
exciting, excellent and exquisite. Supposing
we play on the sound of that X, removing
the E …'

X is for Xciting, Xcellent and Xquisite.
Y is for Yarmouth, it's time that you visit!

The room was filled with acrobatic, bicycle-
riding teddy bears, dancing dolls, roaring toy
lions, splashing swimmers, playful puppets,
leaping fairground horses and cartwheeling

clowns. Edward Elephant flapped his ears and swished his trunk. Victoria performed her tightrope act. They were having so much fun until …

'Oh, we've forgotten the last letter. What about Z?' asked Victoria.

'Oh dear,' said Edward Elephant. 'I can't think of anything. I hope we haven't made an entire alphabet circus only to fall at the last hurdle. A is for *almost*. Oh, Victoria, we must be able to think of something that begins with Z.'

Suddenly, Nanny and Mum's chatting voices came from outside the door. The toys stopped playing and became still and quiet. Victoria rushed to the door full of glee. 'I made an imaginary circus using the whole alphabet, well … *almost*.'

She had only opened the door a creak when she heard that Nanny sounded very worried. 'My plans are ruined!' Nanny told Mum. 'I was going to go to the Hippodrome tonight but their lead clown has come down with a sudden case of stage fright. Now he can't perform at all. He never saw those nerves coming, they snuck up behind him like a silent E. You just never know when stage fright will *strike*.'

'Oh dear,' said Mum, 'does that mean the show will have to be cancelled?'

'I'm afraid so,' said Nanny, 'unless another clown can step in and perform.'

Victoria burst through the door. 'I'm another clown. That is, I'm Victoria Clown. I'll step in and perform.'

'Thank goodness,' said Mum. 'Quick, let's go to the Hippodrome.'

At the Hippodrome, a huge audience sat in a circle around the ring. Victoria walked the tightrope while juggling, and dived into the water spectacle. She rose from the water to find that …

A is for Applause.
B is for Bow.
C is for Clever Victoria.

Victoria blinked through the bright spotlights and saw that the audience in their seats may well have been her toys with Mum and Nanny cheering and whistling. The tightrope may well have been her skipping rope on the ground. The water spectacle may well have been her blue rug. And she may well have just created the most amazing imaginary alphabet circus ever there was.

That night, snuggled up in bed with Edward Elephant, Victoria thought about her day.

'Wow, today was such an adventure. Just think, Edward Elephant, we can make an amazing imaginary alphabet circus tomorrow. So many words, so many ideas. No alphabet circus will ever be the same.'

'Wonderful,' came the very tired, muffled voice of Edward Elephant from under the cosy blanket. 'But for now, let's pretend to be like the silent E and stay shush. I'm so sleepy.'

He curled up and just as he was dozing off …

'Edward Elephant?'

'Yes, Victoria?'

'I've thought of something for Z.'

'Have you now?'

'It's the noise that sleepy circus performers make at bedtime.'

'And what noise might that be?'

'Zzzzzzz.'

FABULOUS FOOTNOTES

On St George's Road in Great Yarmouth you can see the Hippodrome decorated with the swirling patterns of Art Nouveau. The Hippodrome was built in 1903 for the showman George Gilbert. It was 'purpose-built', meaning that George Gilbert jolly well built it on purpose, the very purpose of which was that of a circus. Entertainment was big business in Edwardian times. 1844, that's the Victorian era, saw the arrival of the railways in Great Yarmouth and so people often travelled there for day trips and holidays for seaside fun and entertainment attractions. Should you walk along St George's Street, imagine all the circus music and noise that would have drifted from the doors on to the street.

In the archives at Norfolk Heritage Centre I found lots of circus posters from Victorian and Edwardian times.

As well as the Great Yarmouth Hippodrome, there was also a hippodrome in Norwich. Some of the posters advertised performances in Victoria Gardens and at Castlemeadow, Norwich. You can also see seaside and circus items at the Time and Tide Museum in Yarmouth. These are the landmarks and artefacts that inspired this imaginary story. There's lots of inspiration for your very own imaginary alphabet circus. Now, how would that go?

THE SPECTACULAR STAR OF NORWICH MARKET

Norwich Market was a razzle-dazzle rainbow site,
stalls of many stripes, garish and bright
Fruit and vegetables for sale, fresh and ripe,
fashion's latest handbag caused quite the hype,
fish for sale, salty, crisp with the smell of the sea
and the chitter-chatter queue outside the
chippy was
the place to be!

When skies were blue and the sun shone for days
flower stalls tickled noses with a sweet
enticing haze.

In winter, snowflakes danced, folks wrapped
up warm and toasty
buying books to snuggle up with and
chestnuts, hot and roasty.

Overlooking Norwich Market stood City Hall
A building on St Peter's Street,
very grand and tall,
It's opening received a royal visit from the queen
Crowds gathered for this historic and very
exciting scene.

Above, look up to a night sky where moon and
stars are met.
A little star watches our scene, it's like a
theatre set.
Soon he will discover the magic of a
Christmas eve,
What happens when you make a wish and
dare to believe.

A tale of how a little star comes to find his shine
And so it begins with once upon a time ...

Once upon a time, way up high in a swirling night sky of misty blue and majestic purple, there glistened a little star. And well there might! For what should a star do in the night sky but glisten? Nothing unusual about that. Nothing, that is, except that this little star had a very important purpose. This little star was born to bring people together. But this little star didn't know that. All Little Star knew was that he sat in the same spot in the same sky forever and ever, all by himself, and he felt very lonely. Thousands of other stars sparkled around him like dazzling gems and so he was hardly short of company. But those stars were in groups, and they worked together to make pretty patterns and curious constellations. All alone, Little Star felt very left-out. Why wasn't he part of a group?

Now, if you had told Little Star that he had an important purpose, to bring people together, he would never have believed you, not even after a million moonlit nights! How could he possibly bring people together when he was separate from all the other stars and a long way off from the people down below? Little Star felt very small and insignificant. The only thing that cheered him up was to watch Norwich market. Now, stars usually sleep during the day so that at night they can wake up well rested and ready to shine bright. But Little Star stayed awake all sunlight long; occasionally he drifted off for a quick forty winks but woke up by the thirty-sixth wink as he didn't want to miss a moment of that marketplace.

'Right, ladies and gents, what have I got for you? Fine crockery, form an orderly queue! I'm not just going to give you one plate, oh no, I'm gonna throw in a whole set for the reasonable price of ...'

'Strawberries, sweet and juicy as they get, threepence a punnet!'

'Pots and pans, get ya pots and pans!'

'Fish, fresh fish! And a mug-a-cockles!'

'Books old and new, gather round now, gather round!'

Over the many years Little Star had watched Norwich market, he had seen all sorts of exciting things. He had seen the market with all its stalls knocked down and rebuilt to look bright and impressive. He had seen the construction of a brand new building called City Hall, which stood on St Peter's Street overlooking the market. One autumn in the 1930s he had seen a great opening ceremony for City Hall when Queen Elizabeth paid Norwich a right royal visit – lots of people gathered to watch, it was a very proud and joyful day for everyone to celebrate their fine city.

Magnificent buildings were one thing, but best of all Little Star loved to watch the people as they went about their daily lives. He loved to see the very small, ordinary but caring things that people did though they thought no one noticed. The child who picked up a lady's scarf when it fell from her shoulders, the family who helped an elderly gentleman to carry his groceries, the stallholder who ran after a busy mum who dropped her purse. It was those small acts of kindness that made Little Star feel like the marketplace below was very special. He wished that he could go down and tell people to keep on being kind to each other, as you never know when little stars might be watching. Indeed, more than anything Little Star wished that he could be among the people at Norwich market. He could never feel lonely amid all that kindness.

One winter's night, way up high in a swirling night sky of misty blue and majestic purple, Little Star made a wish. He wished and wished and wished that he could join the people at Norwich market. How it was possible for stars to be among people during the day, Little Star had no idea. It seemed impossible, but ... worth a try. Worth a try. Clocks struck twelve in the world down below. Now midnight is magical at the best of times; on any ordinary midnight an extraordinary thing could happen, but this particular midnight was especially special and so an extra extraordinary thing could happen. You see, this was the midnight of Christmas Eve, the night before Christmas Day. All of a sudden, clear out of the blue and without so much as an 'Excuse me please, magic coming through,' there came a *whoosh*! Something whizzed through the air, powerful as a bolt of lighting. Little Star was so surprised, it was all he could do to gaze in wonder at the big thing that raced by.

'Oh my giddy goodness,' thought Little Star, 'what in this bright and brilliant world is that? It looks like a great big … a great big … a great big … sleigh?'

Yes, indeed, it really was a sleigh. A great big sleigh flying through the air. Swift as the whip of the winter's wind the sleigh soared with marvellous elegance. And well it might, because it was being pulled by some very graceful creatures. Reindeer! Little Star almost span a cartwheel in amazement: he wasn't imagining things, there were reindeer in the sky! They circled around Little Star. In the driver's seat of the sleigh sat an elderly man with a round, jolly face, rosy red cheeks and a merry glint in his eyes. Little Star immediately felt very comforted and happy to see such warmth and joy. Inside the sleigh the man was surrounded by bright bundles of colourful gift boxes wrapped in spotty dotty paper and tied with ribbons.

'Merry Christmas to you, Little Star!'

As the sleigh glided past him one of the reindeer's hooves brushed against Little Star. It was only a gentle nudge but forceful enough to knock Little Star sideways from the spot where he sat in the sky. The next thing Little Star knew he was falling, falling, falling, down, down, down. Light as a feather that drifts from a bird's wing, the sensation of falling was very soft.

'Wheeee!' cried Little Star. 'Down I go, down to the world below. Wheeee! I'm going down to Norwich market to be among all the people, my wish has come true. Wheeee!'

Finally, plop! Little Star landed on something soft and prickly. What could this be? A tree? Surely not. Little Star looked down to see that, indeed, he had landed right on top of a tree. 'Oh no,' thought Little Star, 'there are no trees growing in the marketplace. I must have landed in a forest, a dark forest full of trees and now I'll never be among the people or see Norwich market ever again.' Disappointed as can be, his starry glow grew dimmer and dimmer until it went out completely. Full of sadness, Little Star sank into a deep sleep.

'Merry Christmas to you! Merry Christmas to you!'

Little Star woke slowly to the sound of jolly singing. Who was singing in the middle of a dark forest? Looking down from his perch at the very top of the tall tree, Little Star nearly span a cartwheel of amazement to see such a sight. Around the tree stood a circle of people all wrapped in coats, hats and scarves, holding hands and singing joyfully. The tree itself was covered with delightful decorations, glistening baubles of red, green and gold, candy sticks ... and what was that smell? Gingerbread. Cinnamon. Oranges. This is no ordinary forest, thought Little Star, it must be a magic forest where people hold hands and sing round sparkly trees. He looked around and saw not a magic forest, but something even better ... Norwich market!

There was the razzle-dazzle rainbow site of stalls with many stripes, garish and bright. Some of the stalls were covered with a gentle dusting of snow. Behind him stood City Hall and so Little Star realised that he must be on St Peter's Street.

'Look, Dad,' said a little girl, sitting on her dad's shoulders, 'look at that spectacular star on top of our Christmas tree!'

A Christmas tree, marvelled Little Star. A very special tree that brings people together and I'm sitting right on top of it! A tree in the middle of the city where stars can shine, even in the day time. And so Little Star did just that. He began to shine, brighter and brighter than ever before until everything around him glowed with golden light.

That night Little Star stared way up high to a swirling night sky of misty blue and majestic purple. Those groups of stars really did a wonderful job of working together to make pretty patterns and curious constellations. admired their teamwork, Little Star that there was never any need for

him to have felt small and insignificant just because he didn't fit in with a group. He might have been different but he still had a very important purpose. Every little star has a time to shine.

FABULOUS FOOTNOTES

Should you take a walk along St Peters' Street, Norwich, you can see City Hall, guarded by two fierce lion statues. You can also see Norwich market with its many brightly striped stalls – one of Norwich's most iconic sights. This story is set in the 1950s, when the market was already rich with history. In Saxon times there was a market in Tombland and today's market site dates all the way back to Norman times. Throughout medieval, Tudor and Stuart times, the market was a busy and thriving part of Norwich. As we learned from Little Star, in the 1930s Queen Elizabeth, wife of King George VI, visited Norwich for the opening of City Hall. The marketplace had been knocked down and rebuilt so that it could look as splendid and impressive as City Hall.

In 2005 the market was given another fresh look, and so, these days, the stalls are more modern but the wonderful sense of community has remained. At Norfolk Heritage Centre, I looked at black and white photographs of Norwich market from the 1930s and 1950s. The market looks a busy place, bustling with people and energy. It's amazing how much life can be captured with a single image. These were the landmarks and objects that inspired this imaginary story. Have you ever looked at a photograph and felt inspired to write a story?

8

OSCAR OWL'S SONG OF HOLT

In Appleyard Court outside the bookshop
the animals gather for The Story Stop.
Oscar Owl, friendly, wise and full of knowledge
tells tales of local history in Norfolk and Norwich.
Snuggled on a blanket, dogs, cats and birds
Listen to tales retold in Oscar Owl's words.
Now he sings a song of Holt, told in rhyme
And so it begins with once upon a time …

The streets of Holt are rich with history
it's part of our town's charm and mystery.
Long ago a great fire swept the town;
many of the medieval buildings burned down.
The Georgians rebuilt the town in exquisite style;
fine Georgian buildings interlace every mile.

Pineapples, a sign of wealth in the Georgian age
decorated gateposts, height of fashion, all the rage!
Spot an obelisk at Jacob's Place
topped with a stone pineapple of pomp and grace.

The High Street, outside a shop is the happy home
of a great lion made of stone.
He once guarded Lion House, I wonder if at night
the sight of this lion gave visitors a fright!

On White Lion Street, behold a beautiful view
of Nelson House, a fine building of blue.
Admiral Lord Nelson is a Norfolk figure of note
He sailed the seas and won battles on his boat.

At the heart of the marketplace,
a landmark of respect:
a war memorial, lest we forget.
Soldiers who fought in the First and
Second World War
are remembered here, now and forever more.

Along the High Street near the marketplace's heart
glimmers a marvellous work of art.
A millennium clock of blue and gold
links two buildings, now the new joins with the old.

Those who visit Holt and take time to explore
will see these astonishing sites and more.
In our lovely Holt, it comes as no surprise
that we are celebrated for our north Norfolk skies!

FABULOUS FOOTNOTES

Take a stroll along the High Street in Holt and you will see an ancient relative of Oscar Owl. A wooden statue of an owl marks the legend of the Holt Owl, which mysteriously flew in and out of Holt, long ago. As you walk along a modern high street of shops and cafes you will notice that some of the buildings are of Georgian style. This is because in 1708 a great fire swept Holt. As many of the medieval buildings burned down, the Georgians then rebuilt the town in their elegant style. You may spot all the sights regaled to us by Oscar Owl, all dating to different periods of history. There is even a Holt Owl Trail that you can follow. These are the landmarks and sights that inspired this imaginary story. Which one of Oscar Owl's sights would you make up a story about?

9

THE RAZZLE-DAZZLE RAINBOW STORY DRESS

Serena, Serena was a day dreamer
With stories she decided to weave
a story dress with rainbow sleeves
Stitches and dreams, stitches and dreams
Serena sewed stories into the seams
Snapdragon wings, a Tudor rose
Tightrope strings and a clown's nose
Market stripes and King's Lynn fishes
Circus delights and fairground wishes
Stitches and dreams, stitches and dreams
Serena sewed stories into the seams
Stitching in time, this story saves nine
And so it begins with once upon a time ...

Once upon a time – a modern time, could have happened last Friday sort of a time – a girl called Serena won a very special school prize. No, it wasn't the prize for gazing out of the window and daydreaming, a genuine prize her teacher Miss Rose had suggested the class invent just for Serena. It wasn't that Serena didn't want to listen, it's just that she absolutely loved nothing more than to dream up ideas for fashion designs and theatre costumes that she was going to make.

Serena had an extraordinary talent for sewing. Being rather a shy and thoughtful girl, Serena enjoyed the quiet, concentrated time that sewing gave her, time alone to think and be creative. But there was always time for friends. Serena loved spending time with her best friend Rhiannon, who was a writer extraordinaire, penning plays and poems with her rainbow pencils, a different coloured pencil for every day of the week. Outside of school, the two were nearly always round each other's houses, Serena stitching and

Rhiannon scribbling. In class they often sat next to each other and Serena was grateful for Rhiannon's help when the class had to get their books out. Serena needed to take her time when she was reading and writing a bit more than the other children in her class. Miss Rose, her teacher, was very kind and encouraged Serena to ask for help when she needed it.

Serena had no idea that asking for help could be so hilarious – a small group of her classmates would always laugh at her and sing in mocking voices 'Miss Rose, Miss Rose, I can't do it.' Just because they were faster than her! Mum told Serena not to pay any attention to those silly bullies. Serena thought that was easier said than done. It wasn't too much trouble to ignore them when they laughed at her from across the classroom. The real problem was that those mocking voices followed her around wherever she went. Even when she was at home the voices followed her. 'Miss Rose, Miss Rose, I can't do it.'

One Friday Serena and her classmates were at Norfolk Heritage Centre. They were on a school trip looking at all the curious and delightful objects in the archives. They looked at maps of Norfolk from all different periods of history, old black and white photographs of the area and some very old books and catalogues. When they got back to school Miss Rose told everyone that the homework over the weekend was to 'make a story. A story about the streets of Norfolk over the years, inspired by the items we saw in Norfolk Heritage Centre. We will share our stories on Monday. There's a history prize up for grabs, we'll have a vote on who we think should win in class.'

Serena began to worry until she felt dizzy. She had never written a story before. How was she going to do it in just one weekend? Of course, she knew that she could ask Miss Rose for help. But then she heard the bullies' voices: 'Miss Rose, Miss Rose, I can't do it.' Serena stayed quiet. Later that afternoon she was at drama club with Rhiannon.

'I'm so excited about the school homework,' Rhiannon said. 'I love writing stories! I've sharpened all my best rainbow pencils. I'm going to write an epic time travel novel. Look!' she thrust her scribble-covered scrapbook in front of Serena. Pages and pages of writing. Serena felt dizzy with worry again. 'Oh, that's wonderful, Rhiannon.' She knew that her friend had no idea how she was feeling and wasn't trying to be mean or anything, she just wanted to share her enthusiasm. All the same, Serena couldn't help but feel that she wanted to be left alone. Then it struck her that of course, she could ask Rhiannon for help. After all, that's what friends are for. But then she heard the bullies' voices: 'Miss Rose, Miss Rose, I can't do it.' Serena stayed quiet. That evening at home Serena sat with her mum at the dinner table. She told Mum all about the school trip to Norfolk Heritage Centre and the homework to make a story.

'That sounds like a fun challenge,' said Mum. 'Yes it is,' said Serena. She wanted to tell her mum that she felt worried to the point of dizziness. She knew that Mum would help her with the homework if only she explained how she felt and asked for help. But then she heard the bullies' voices: 'Miss Rose, Miss Rose, I can't do it.' Serena stayed quiet yet again.

The next morning, Saturday, Serena was at home sewing. She had surrounded herself with her favourite bits and bobs of fabric in the hope that sewing would help her feel calm. But no, she was still worrying and worrying. 'Make a story' – the words played over and over in her head, they filled her with dread. 'Make a story, make a story, make a ... wait a minute. *Make* a story!' This time, the words felt different, uplifting, exciting. 'Miss Rose said *make* a story. She didn't say write a story. She said *make* a story. That means I could make a dress, a story dress. A theatre costume inspired by local history. The first thing I'll do is make a simple, plain dress then sew all my ideas on to it. A blank canvas for creative fun!'

Once the simple, plain dress was complete, Serena decided to make a list of all the history she would include. As she neatly penned a very detailed list, Serena was so transfixed on the task ahead that she didn't even notice the ease with which she was writing without worrying about it.

'At Norfolk Heritage Centre we looked at lots of maps.' Now, how to put a map on a dress? Serena sewed lots of winding street patterns all over the dress.

Stitches and dreams, stitches and dreams, Serena sewed stories into the seams.

'We looked at old copies of *The Norfolk Chronicle* from the Georgian era and saw an advertisement for a show at the Theatre Royal.' Now, how to represent the theatre on a dress? Serena made two long flowing red sleeves which she draped across either side of the dress. She interwove a little rope into the sleeves and fastened it at the back. Once you pulled the little rope, the sleeves would part like the opening of theatre curtains.

Stitches and dreams, stitches and dreams, Serena sewed stories into the seams.

'What next? We saw magazine articles and catalogues about the Savages of King's Lynn who made super-fun fairground rides for Victorian families.' Serena outlined jumping fairground horses on to some gold fabric and sewed them on to the dress.

Stitches and dreams, stitches and dreams, Serena sewed stories into the seams.

'We looked at books about the brave fisherfolk of King's Lynn who sailed the stormy seas on boats.' Serena cut out shapes of boats and fish on to some blue fabric and sewed them on to the dress.

Stitches and dreams, stitches and dreams, Serena sewed stories into the seams.

'We looked at old books with pictures of fierce but friendly medieval snapdragons.' Serena cut some dragon wings from bits of glistening green fabric. She attached the dragon wings to the dress.

Stitches and dreams, stitches and dreams, Serena sewed stories into the seams.

'We got swept away on Wymondham's brush-making and woodturning history.' Serena collected some twigs together to represent brushes. She made a necklace from the twigs and hung it around the neckline of the dress.

Stitches and dreams, stitches and dreams, Serena sewed stories into the seams.

'We looked at maps which showed the magnificent procession of Queen Elizabeth I who rode a grand horse through a gate of Tudor roses.' Serena sewed a bright Tudor rose at the top of the dress, just under the neckline in the middle of the twig necklace. The rose had red petals on the outside, white petals on the inside and a yellow dot in the middle.

Stitches and dreams, stitches and dreams, Serena sewed stories into the seams.

'We looked at circus posters with pictures of tumbling, juggling, colourful clowns walking tightropes.' Serena took some red bobbles for clown noses and sewed them around the hem of the dress. She sewed dangling strings along the sleeves to represent tightropes. She sewed some swirling Art Nouveau patterns around the skirt.

Stitches and dreams, stitches and dreams, Serena sewed stories into the seams.

'We looked at old photographs of Norwich market with those wonderful striped stalls – what a lively place to go shopping!' Serena sewed colourful stripes of red, yellow and blue across the dress to represent Norwich market.

Stitches and dreams, stitches and dreams, Serena sewed stories into the seams.

'We learned about the legend of the Holt Owl, which mysteriously flew in and out of Holt, one dark night.' Serena cut out some pieces of fabric to look like feathers and dotted them around the dress. Then she stitched some stars and swirling clouds to represent the beautiful north Norfolk skies through which the owl flew.

Stitches and dreams, stitches and dreams, Serena sewed stories into the seams.

The finished product was a razzle-dazzle story dress of wondrous delights. But no, it wasn't quite complete yet, something was missing. Something from the modern day. Serena thought of Rhiannon, who loved to write with her rainbow pencils. 'Yes, that's what I'll add, something to represent my friend.'

Serena sewed rainbow colours across the sleeves. Now *that* is a Razzle-Dazzle Rainbow Story Dress.

On Monday morning, the classroom assembled to share their stories. Serena wasn't the only one to make something. Some of her classmates had written songs and played pieces of music inspired by local history. Lots of pictures, poems and pieces of writing were plastered across the walls. Rhiannon had, of course, written an entire dramatic page-turner of a time travel novel which she was very excited to share an extract from. But the story that caught the most attention from the class was …

The Razzle-Dazzle Rainbow Story Dress.

'Wow, wow, wow, just look at that dress!'

'That's very creative and imaginative, Serena,' said Miss Rose. 'You've really thought about all the history we learned. Such beautiful attention to detail. I can see you've thought about the dazzling Georgian Theatre Royal, the Wymondham brushes, the medieval snapdragons, the Victorian fairground animals, Tudor Norwich, the spectacular Edwardian circus, the 1950s Norwich market, the owl of Holt and the streets, seas and skies of Norfolk. But what do the rainbow sleeves represent?'

'They represent my best friend Rhiannon,' said Serena. 'She loves to write with her rainbow pencils. I wanted to choose something from the modern day and well, friendship seemed like a great idea.'

'That's wonderful,' said Miss Rose. 'Let's put this dress at the front of the classroom on display for everyone to see. Well done Serena, you should be proud.'

The class voted for Serena to win the history prize.

'Thank you, everyone' said Serena. 'One day I'm going to make costumes for the theatre.'

'Excellent,' said Miss Rose, 'and wouldn't it be exciting if you could write your own plays and design the costumes for them?'

That got Serena thinking, it seemed a shame that the bullies had intimidated her to the point where she was entirely put off writing. She wanted to write and felt she'd be good at it given the time. Serena decided to embrace the challenge.

'I'm going to write the tale of *The Story Dress*, she thought. 'I've never done this before. I don't know how long it will take me or how it's going to turn out but I'm going to try. What's more I'm going to ask for help.'

Serena turned to her friend. 'Rhiannon, will you please help me to write my story?'

'Ooo!' Rhiannon squealed with excitement. 'Yes, of course I'll help you. And please can we underline the titles? A chance to use my rainbow ruler!'

After school that day the two friends went to Serena's house. Mum was very happy to hear that Serena's story dress had been a huge success. Serena felt much more confident to get out her pencil and scrapbook to write. Until, that is, she opened up a blank page.

'Oh dear,' she said to Rhiannon. 'This could take a long while.'

'Good,' said Rhiannon 'I needed some time to colour co-ordinate my pencils and rubbers.

Just write whatever you want and I'm here if you need help.'

'I don't know where to start,' Serena worried.

'Just write down the first words that spring to mind,' Rhiannon said.

Serena wrote down the first words that sprang to mind: 'Miss Rose, Miss Rose, I can't do it.'

Rhiannon peered over. 'Great writing,' she said, 'you've just got the apostrophe and the 't' in the wrong place.'

Serena flung her hand to her forehead. 'See, I knew I couldn't do it, I'm so rubbish at …'

Rhiannon leaned across and rubbed out the apostrophe and the 't' with her rainbow rubber. 'That looks like a better place to start. Why don't you take it from there?'

Serena looked at the new start to her story.
Miss Rose, Miss Rose, I can do it.

FABULOUS FOOTNOTES

Serena has sewn together all the different landmarks and objects that inspired the imaginary stories in this book. Now, how would you make a story?